A REASON TO LIVE

A REASON TO LOVE SERIES: BOOK 1

T.K. CHAPIN

WWW.TKCHAPIN.COM

Branch Publishing

To claim a FREE Christian Romance visit offer.tkchapin.com

Version: 12.12.2018

ISBN: 1717929150

ISBN-13: 978-1717929150

Dedicated to my loving wife.
For all the years she has put up with me
And many more to come.

CONTENTS

CHAPTER 1

$\mathcal{P}$OUNDING COMING FROM THE FRONT door of his house on the South Hill woke Jonathan Dunken from sleep at three o'clock in the morning. Then the doorbell chimed, pulling him further away from his slumber and fully awake. He had only been asleep for an hour, as he had been up late the night before sketching building concepts for a client. He was the co-founder and sole architect of his and his brother Tyler's company, *Willow Design*. A company the two of them started just a few years ago, after Marie passed and Jonathan needed more work to throw himself into.

Pushing his eyelids open, he sat up in his bed, smoothing a hand over his face. *Who on earth is that?* He wondered. The doorbell chimed again, and he begrudgingly emerged from his bed and left his bedroom.

He traveled out from his room, through the long hallway, and down the glass stairs. As he entered the foyer, more pounding on the door sounded, edging his already growing irritation. He was ready to rip into whoever was on the other side of that door. But when he finally opened it, his heart plunged and the wind fanning his anger fell quiet. It was his sister-in-law, Shawna Gillshock, a woman he hadn't seen since the funeral four years ago.

Shawna looked just like he remembered her—a mess, her brunette hair disheveled, eyeliner mingled with rainwater ran down each of her cheeks. She was wearing a stained pair of ragged sweats three times too big and a ragged oversized hooded sweatshirt. He immediately noticed the sight of fresh blood on a cut near her left eyebrow.

"I need your help, Jonathan. I didn't know where else to go." Her voice was strained, filled with desperation. She jerked her head toward the car in the driveway. Sheets of rain and wind whipped back and forth in the night's air, dancing across the headlights of the car. "My dad wouldn't let me come to his house. I need a place for me and my daughter, Rose, to stay tonight. My boyfriend beat me again, and I'm leaving him for good this time. You're the only person I know that he doesn't know. Please?"

Jonathan was moved with compassion, though a part of him wanted to say 'no' to her. Deep down, somewhere beneath the pain and grief that followed losing his wife, he heard a whisper and felt a nudge. *Let her stay.*

"Okay. You can stay." He helped her inside with her luggage and daughter. The luggage she had brought didn't consist of much. A backpack and one suitcase. Once the two of them had everything inside the house in the foyer, he led the way to the guest room on the main floor of the two-story house. The room was tucked away at the end of the hallway. Opening the door, he flipped on the light switch. Two lamps, one on each nightstand on either side of the bed, turned on. Each of the nightstands, along with the dresser and crown molding, was stark white. The walls were a warm brown, not dark, but not light either. On the far side of the bedroom, near the dresser, was another doorway leading into an en-suite bathroom.

"Thank you so much for this." Her words were filled with genuine gratitude as she set her backpack on the bed. She turned and glanced at the TV on top of the dresser.

"How long do you think you'll be here, Shawna?" Jonathan was gently reminding her it wasn't a long-term solution but more of a friendly gesture in a time of need.

"Just a few days. I'm going to call my dad again tomorrow and see if I can convince him to let us stay there with him and Betty until I can figure something out."

The mention of her parents jogged painful memories that Jonathan had tried to forget. His parents had died his senior year of high school, so he only really had Marie's parents in his life. "Okay, and if he doesn't budge?"

Shawna turned to face him. "I'll figure something out. Don't worry about me, just thanks again for tonight."

Her daughter became fussy a moment later, a whimper escaping. "What's wrong, Rose?"

She touched her tummy. "I'm hungry."

"How old is she?"

Smiling, Shawna turned to him. "She's two. Talking away already. Do you have anything she can eat?"

Scrambling through the fridge in his mind, he shrugged. "Does she like tuna?"

"Um, not really. Do you have hot dogs, macaroni, or something more kid-friendly like that?"

"No, but there are eggs in the fridge. Sorry. I wasn't really prepared for you." He tipped a smile, trying to loosen the awkwardness and embrace the disturbance of the entire situation.

She laughed lightly. "It's totally fine. Eggs work great. She loves scrambled eggs. Thank you again, Jonathan. It means the world that you took us in tonight."

"Don't mention it. Do you need help cooking, or can you manage it?"

"It's pretty basic. I think I got it handled. You look like you need some sleep, so go ahead."

"I do need sleep. Going back to bed now. 'Night."

Leaving Shawna and Rose in the guest room, he shut the door quietly and thought of his late wife, Marie, as he made his way back to his bedroom upstairs. Shawna was his only sister-in-law, and she had made frequent appearances in his and Marie's life, but that had been years ago. Even back in the day, Shawna was always in need. Her life reminded him of a slow-moving train wreck in progress. Though her life was a wreck, Marie was always ready and willing to love on her and care for her when she was in need of her big sister. That was Marie's nature with not only family, but anyone who was in need.

CHAPTER 2

JONATHAN - AGE 25

OASTING GLASSES OF SPARKLING CIDER while a fire roared in the fireplace, Jonathan pulled Marie in close to him. His mouth tipped a smile as he peered into her inviting green eyes. "To us and our first home, my love."

The glasses clinked together, and they both sipped. Marie set her glass down on the coffee table and sat down on the couch. Jonathan joined her. She beamed as she turned her body fully toward him and leaned forward. "You're the best husband a wife can ask for. Did you know that?"

He set his glass down beside hers and then moved across the couch and over her. She let herself sink into the couch as he crawled on top of her, holding himself up by his hands. A smile curling both corners of his mouth, he felt love as he peered into her eyes. They had a connection that went beyond words, beyond a simple 'I love you.' Kissing her, he stopped and brought his lips near her ear. "You're the best wife. You bring sunshine into an otherwise dark world."

They kissed.

Deepening the kiss, Jonathan placed his hand on her hip,

then slid it up her side. Her back arched. Moving his hand again to her hip, he slipped his hand beneath her shirt, his fingers lightly gliding across her side.

The doorbell rang, bringing their moment to an abrupt stop.

Sitting up, Marie hugged herself with her arms and flashed a look of bewilderment at Jonathan.

"Who is that? It's almost ten o'clock." Jonathan arose from the couch and walked to the front door to answer it. He checked the peep hole. It was Shawna, his sister-in-law. His insides ached knowing the romantic evening with his beloved was over before it had officially begun.

Marie lifted herself from the couch and came to him at the door. Placing a hand on the small of his back, she peered up at him. "I know that look. It's Shawna, isn't it?"

Jonathan turned to his wife and lowered his voice. "Yes, but can't we just not answer this *one* time?"

"*Jonathan*. We are to imitate Christ, aren't we?" Reaching past him, she grabbed hold of the door handle and opened it. Marie was a devout wife, but not to a fault. She knew God came first and she wasn't afraid to remind Jonathan of it when he needed reminding.

A broken Shawna stood on the porch of their new house. "He broke my heart! I can't believe it. I thought this one was different!"

They continued talking in low voices as Marie led her inside. Jonathan took the glasses of sparkling cider into the kitchen. He was annoyed about her sister showing up, but there wasn't much he could do about it. As he prepared coffee for the two of them, he wondered how long she'd be sticking around this time. She had a pattern. After a day, sometimes a few, she'd end up talking to whatever boyfriend had upset her and then go right back to the same guy who'd broken her heart into a million pieces.

Returning to the living room, Jonathan handed them both a cup of coffee.

"Thanks, Jonathan." Shawna took the warm beverage quickly and brought it to her lips for a drink. Marie, however, only took a sip and set it down. She then pressed in on more conversation with her sister. It fascinated Jonathan how she could listen to the same issues and stories over and over again and care deeply each time. He knew one thing for certain—Marie definitely had more of the Spirit of Christ within her than he did. That was one of the reasons he'd fallen so deeply in love with Marie. She had always made him want to be a better man, a better person, just by the way she was.

TWO WEEKS LATER, Shawna was still living with them in their new home. Jonathan decided to speak with Marie about asking Shawna to leave. He did it over a candlelit dinner on the back patio of their house one evening when he got off work early from the design firm. He cooked her favorite meal, seafood Alfredo, and even bought a bouquet of flowers. He thought he could sneak all the romance in without her knowing he was up to something.

Setting her fork down after eating, she wiped her mouth with the napkin and smiled at him across the table. "You can't fool me, Jonathan. I know you too well. What's all this about?"

He swallowed the lump of anxiety in his throat. Gaze gliding over to the sliding glass door into the house, he looked back at Marie. "Don't you think it's about time for Shawna to leave? She's not looking for a job and there's zero movement going on with her."

Marie got quiet. That quietness was the quietness

Jonathan knew all too well. She closed her eyes for a moment —he suspected she was praying—then opened them. "Jonathan, I love you. I love my sister too. She is trying to start a new life without the abuse. She's been going to church with us, and I really think it's helping her by staying with us."

"I get that, but—"

Marie interrupted. "But, what?" She shook her head. "Remember God's love for us, Jonathan. It's unconditional and it never runs out. We need to extend that the best we can. I totally agree that if she starts seeing that man again or shows signs of drug use, she has to leave. But until then, I feel it's okay. If you strongly disagree with it, that's fine. She can leave. I don't want to cause issues in our marriage. I will do whatever you ultimately wish to do, but I can't help but state my view on the matter."

Jonathan's heart couldn't help but be moved by the compassion and gentleness of his wife. She disagreed with him, yet would submit if it came to it. "You're right about God's love, Marie. I guess I just need to focus on the good. She isn't with him and she's doing the right things in life."

Two days later, Marie found a pipe in one of her sister's jean pockets and showed it to Jonathan. With tears in her eyes, Marie showed her the door. Holding his wife close to him after his sister-in-law left, Jonathan kissed the brow of his wife's forehead and thanked her for doing the right thing. The two of them spent the rest of that particular evening praying for Shawna and reading their Bible together. They weren't sure where Shawna would end up that evening, or the nights following, but they let the Lord comfort their broken hearts and their faith comforted them.

CHAPTER 3

*E*ARLY THE NEXT MORNING, JONATHAN forced himself out of bed and down the hallway to his exercise room. With nothing but a pair of jogging pants on and a pair of worn running shoes, he climbed onto the treadmill and started in on his routine. He jogged for an hour every morning and thirty minutes every night. In the mornings, if he was feeling in the mood, he'd hit the weights for an hour after his jog. Exercise and fitness were the way Jonathan kept his mind sharp and his body in shape while still maintaining a sedentary job. Without work and exercise, he probably wouldn't be here today, or at least not the man he had become.

Ten minutes into his jog, he grabbed the stereo remote from the cup holder of the treadmill and flipped on the classic rock station. With each step in stride with the beat, he worked up to a high speed. Sweat began to pour from his chest, sides, and face.

Jonathan was forty-five minutes into the jog when suddenly, he heard a crash come from downstairs. Pausing the treadmill and the radio, he listened for it again as he panted from being out of breath. Another clash, and this time he could hear pots and pans clanking against one another. Grabbing for the towel hanging on the arm of the treadmill, he patted his face and stepped off the equipment. Leaving the room, he continued to hear the sounds coming from downstairs. He grabbed a white shirt from his room and put it on as he descended the stairs.

Entering the kitchen, he spotted Rose on the floor with pots in hand. She turned to him and looked up.

"Hi."

"Good morning, Rose. You must be in charge of today's wakeup call?"

"Oh, sorry. Did she wake you?" Shawna walked into the kitchen and over to the table. Sitting down, she pulled out her phone.

"No. I was already up when I heard the clanking." Jonathan approached her at the table and sat down. She looked to be in far better condition than last night. Shawna was wearing a pair of blue jeans and a white t-shirt, and her hair was up in a messy bun. "You sleep well?"

Her mouth tipped into a grin. "Yes, better than I have in a while. I feel great. Such a comfortable bed."

"Good." Jonathan peered over at Rose and smiled. "Would've been nice to meet Rose before today. It's been years, Shawna."

"I know. I wasn't sure if you wanted to meet her though, you know? I don't even know if I'm really your sister-in-law anymore."

Jonathan raised a hand. "It's okay. I understand." He got up and walked over to the coffee pot and pushed an empty Chinese takeout box out of the way. He started to make a pot of coffee. As he poured the grounds and water into the pot, he suddenly became aware of his living conditions all around. Takeout boxes littered the counters, pizza boxes stacked on the far side of the kitchen table. He lived like a slob. Embarrassed, he turned to Shawna.

"Sorry about the mess."

Tipping her chin, she let out a laugh. "It's okay. I'd live like this too if I were alone. I plan to clean it all up today . . . that is, if you don't mind."

Jonathan shook his head. "I can clean up after myself. You don't need to do that."

He came over and sat at the table with her. She shook her head. "No, I want to earn my keep here. Cleaning is the least I can do. Plus, there are some things that need to be put away so Rose doesn't hurt herself."

Recalling the fact that he hadn't helped bring in a crib or bed or highchair, he glanced at Rose, then back at Shawna with a raised eyebrow. "Do you have anything else for her hidden away somewhere in that car? Or somewhere we can go pick it up from?"

Her eyes welled with tears as fear flickered in her eyes. Covering her mouth, she looked at Jonathan. "I didn't have time to grab anything more than a few essentials. She doesn't have her bed or anything here, and I can't go back to that house."

Moved with compassion, he leaned forward and shook his head as he made eye contact with Shawna. "It's okay. We'll get it all from the store today, and it's on my card. Everything is going to be okay for the two of you."

She pushed out a sad smile. "I can't ask you to do that, Jonathan. I don't want you to have to take care of us."

"I insist you let me. I'm more than willing. You know as much as I do that Marie would want it this way."

Her tears dried in her eyes suddenly at the mention of her sister's name. Hope glinted as a genuine smile peeked through her pained expression. "Marie would, wouldn't she?"

"Yes. I believe so. Why don't you make me a list, and I'll

go to the store and get all the stuff we need for Rose? I'll take care of that and you take care of the cleaning. Deal?"

"Deal!" Shawna reached out a hand and the two of them shook.

WAKING THE NEXT DAY, Jonathan ventured downstairs after his workout and shower. He looked forward to speaking with Shawna to see how Rose had done with the toddler bed he'd picked out from the department store and spent a greater portion of an hour assembling last night. When he didn't find the two of them in the kitchen, he ventured down the hallway to the guest room.

Leaning an ear against the door, he could hear Rose chattering away and the TV was turned on. Rapping his knuckles, he gave the door a few light knocks.

"Hey, Shawna. How'd the bed work out last night for Rose? Did she love it?"

Only silence returned. He figured maybe she was in the en-suite bathroom. Turning around, he was about to walk away when the door opened. He turned.

It was Rose.

"Hi."

Getting down to her eye level, he smiled at her. "Good morning, Rose. Is your mom in the bathroom?"

She started saying 'mama' and tried to squeeze past Jonathan in the doorway. Scooping her up into his arms, he pushed open the door. The bathroom door was wide open, nobody inside. Looking around, he saw a note on the made bed. Walking over with Rose perched on his hip, he lifted the handwritten note.

She's better off with you.
Take care of my princess.

Shawna

A woman from CPS with black hair pulled back in a tight ponytail showed up at about a quarter after noon that day. Inviting the woman inside, Jonathan had her sit at the kitchen table while he made Rose lunch. With Rose in her highchair and a peanut butter and jelly sandwich on her tray, Jonathan ventured over and sat with the woman at the table.

"Where is Rose's father?"

Jonathan felt embarrassed. "I have no idea. I didn't know Rose existed until they showed up on my front porch two nights ago."

"And you mentioned on the phone that this is your sister-in-law's child. Where is your wife so I can speak with her?"

Jonathan's heart ached at the request. "I'd love to talk to her too. Unfortunately, she passed away four years ago. It's just me."

The woman's expression softened. "I'm sorry to hear that. I only assumed because you said 'sister-in-law.' Now, Mr. Dunken, I know you're probably wondering what is going to happen to Rose. Since you're family, you can keep her here. Is that something you're interested in doing?"

A sardonic laugh escaped his lips. "What's the alternative?"

"Well, she could be taken and placed in foster care. You do have options, Mr. Dunken."

"Call me Jonathan, please. That's *not* an option, in my mind." Peering over at Rose as she gobbled up a piece of her sandwich, he smiled. "I might not have kids of my own, but that doesn't mean I can't learn and figure it out. After all, that's kind of what parents do anyway, right?" Jonathan put on a brave face in the moment, but he was trembling inside at the thought of being responsible for a tiny human being. He once dreamed of having a child of his own, but that dream had always included a helpmate. Doing it alone terrified him.

"All right . . . if you're sure, I will get started on the temporary guardianship to prevent her from being able to just show up and take Rose. It's obvious that she isn't stable right now. You understand that things can get ugly, Mr. Dunken? I mean, Jonathan?"

"Ugly?" He shook his head. "I'm not following."

"I've seen it a thousand times. The biological parent vanishes for a long time and then re-enters the picture. The guardian has bonded with the child and refuses to give them up. I just had a case where the mom was out of the picture for three years. She didn't care until her sister tried adopting the kids, and now it's a mess. It's in court, and family members are hating one another over the whole situation."

Jonathan raised a hand. "I'm not worried about any of that. None of that family has been in contact with me for years. I hardly think it'll be an issue. All I've done here is take care of a kid who was dropped off on my doorstep."

Rising to her feet, the CPS worker smiled warmly and shook his hand. "You're doing the right thing by taking Rose in."

"Thanks."

Seeing her to the door, Jonathan shut the door and returned to the kitchen where Rose was still sitting in her highchair.

"Guess it's just us two now, kid."

CHAPTER 4

JONATHAN - AGE 27

*G*RASPING A FIRM HOLD OF his wife Marie's hand as they sat on their couch waiting for the pregnancy test, Jonathan knew in his heart what he wanted. For as long as he could remember, Jonathan had an affinity for children. The idea of having one who had Marie's features mixed with his own filled his heart with a joy he didn't know possible. He joked with Marie constantly about not wanting a child if it was a girl, but they both knew he'd be happy with either. They had been trying for over a year to have a baby, ever since they'd first bought their house. It was a natural next step in life, and they were financially ready to take it on.

This particular day was the third time she was late on her monthly, and probably the hundredth time taking a pregnancy test. It was the same every time she would take a test. A lot of excitement, followed by a quiet sadness after a negative result.

"Babe." Marie's tone said it all. It was negative, yet again. They'd agreed that this time, they'd go see a fertility doctor if it was negative. The following week, they did just that. With scheduling conflicts between the lab at the hospital for Jonathan and Marie's OB/GYN appointment, they ended up getting their results at different times but on the same day. Jonathan found out that he was the issue. He was born without his *vas deferens*, the tubes needed to carry the sperm. He didn't know what that meant going forward for them, but he wanted Marie happy, so he bought flowers and was on the way home to tell her they'd figure something out when Marie called him, crying hysterically. She had uterine cancer, and suddenly, his lack of tubes didn't matter, so much so that he didn't even bother to share his own news with her.

Jonathan spent the next few weeks fighting with doctors, or at least it felt that way. Marie had a hysterectomy. She started taking a plethora of cancer medications and immediately started in on chemo. Her chances of living out their dreams of growing old together grew slimmer by the day until they were so thin, they disappeared. Her cancer was growing more aggressive. The news shocked Jonathan and challenged his faith in a way he had never experienced before in his life. *How could God do this to us?* was a continuous thought in and outside the countless appointments he went to with her.

"I read an article today. Vitamin C infusion treatments. I read online that it has cured cancer, diabetes, and more." Jonathan's suggestion came over dinner one evening.

"Jonathan . . ." The way in which she said his name stung. They both knew reality. There was no way they could afford such a treatment. He had looked at the costs and it was in the thousands. Their insurance wouldn't cover it and their savings account had barely $0.23 in it after all the cancer medications and chemo and hysterectomy. It pained the deepest parts of Jonathan not to be able to provide what could possibly keep his wife alive a little bit longer, or even better, possibly even cure it completely. *Prayer will have to suffice*, Marie kept saying.

This time, Jonathan couldn't contain his silence any longer. He let his pent-up anger and frustration about the situation fire away. "It's just not fair, Marie. We've done almost everything right in our life and marriage, and people who continually scorn God have it better. We just wanted a baby and now your uterus has been surgically removed after it tried to kill you. Now you might soon be dead! All the while, your sister is a drug addict and a loser, and people like your cousin can pop kids out like they're Pez from a Pez dispenser, but good people like us can't even have one?" He paused, hot tears escaping the corners of his eyes. "You're dying, Marie, and I don't know what to do. Marie . . . don't leave me."

Her silence spoke louder than a word could ever accomplish. Her eyes held disappointment in him that stung on the deepest of levels.

Jonathan apologized. "I'm sorry. This world just doesn't make sense. It's so broken."

"That's why everyone needs Jesus, Jonathan. It's only He who can bring us joy. I'm happy with our lives the way that they are. I'm at peace with dying. I'm heartbroken for you and what I will leave behind, but I know where I am going." She shrugged, a smile curling her lips. "God has given me a beautiful life, and Jonathan? I know God has a plan in the midst of all this. Do you?"

Jonathan stood up, angry, not at Marie but at the situation. He walked over to the mantle in their living room and looked at a photograph of the two of them from their wedding day nine years ago. Glancing over at Marie, he was overwhelmed with love for her and it softened his heart in the moment. Even though she was weak from chemo and radiation and knew she was dying, she remained happy, content, and joyful. She always did. That was just how Marie was. Even when her father stopped speaking to her for months after she'd married him, she still held onto joy. Jonathan knew she was better than him in every way. He touched the framed picture, then glanced over at his wife still at the table.

"I'm sorry, Marie. I shouldn't get so worked up about things we have no control over."

She rose to her feet and walked over to Jonathan at the mantle. Leaning up to his face, she planted a kiss on his lips and rested a hand on his chest. "God is in control, and He is *always* good. We can't ever forget that for a moment. It's He who sustains our joy, our happiness, not the outside world or circumstances."

Holding his wife close to him, Jonathan didn't understand the depths of her faith but held on to the hope of one day having a faith like hers. He also hoped that God would heal her, hoped that God wouldn't take the one good thing in his life away.

CHAPTER 5

*J*ONATHAN PLACED ROSE ON THE floor of his study as she had become frightened by the thunderstorm outside. The study sat on the upper floor of the house, across from his studio and beside his bedroom. He conducted all business affairs in the study and his creative endeavors in his studio. The ceilings in the study were vaulted, the walls an olive green, and the beams a dark wood. The wood ran across the ceiling and down each of the walls. Smoky black-colored built-in shelves lined the northern and western walls of his study. Each square inch of the built-ins was filled with books and trinkets he had collected over the years.

After he set Rose down on the hardwood floor, he noticed she didn't pay any attention to the *Elmo's A, B, C* book flopped open and facedown beside her. She also didn't seem to care about the blocks or dolls or any of the other small toys he'd given her to preoccupy her while he tried to work. She had been doing fine with their arrangement over the last week since her mother had left, but she didn't seem fine now.

Maybe she had just been too upset about the storm or maybe it was something else. He wasn't sure. Her little eyes lifted and connected with Jonathan's eyes, piercing his heart. Her eyes glistened, then little tears started to tumble down her cheeks.

"Mama." The word was soft and sad. Then, she began to cry.

Jonathan pushed himself away from his desk and came over to her on the floor. Bending a knee, he did what he had been doing every time she cried for her mom. He rubbed her back in a circular motion and spoke sweet affectionate statements softly to her, attempting to ease the pain. He wasn't sure precisely what she understood about her own circumstances at the moment, but he had a feeling she understood enough for it to hurt. Mom wasn't there anymore, a devastating thought to any child.

The woman from CPS had finalized the temporary guardianship just days ago and had him come into her office to sign. Now there was a court date approaching in the coming months that would suspend Shawna's rights as a parent and place all rights and responsibilities on his shoulders. Jonathan knew it was a heavy burden to take on a child, possibly for the next sixteen years, and one he didn't take lightly. He did something he hadn't done in a while over the last few days. He prayed, even though his heart wasn't fully in it.

After Rose calmed down in his study, he glanced at his watch. It was already going on eight o'clock and he had barely done an hour's worth of work on the proposal he was working on. He had a meeting in three days to deliver the final proposal to Tyler. His brother was the one who dealt with the clients. He had a prettier face, in Jonathan's mind.

Raking his hair with his fingers as the stress of his deadline weighed heavily on his thoughts, Jonathan knew this arrangement needed a change. He just wasn't sure what it was yet. His productivity and quality had suffered greatly since Rose moved in, but he didn't blame her. It wasn't her fault Shawna had skipped out on her. She was just a child who needed love.

KYLIE HAWTHORNE WAS ALREADY RUNNING LATE for her shift at *Ethan's*, a fine dining restaurant in the heart of Spokane, when Grandma Faith called for her to come into the living room for a moment. Scrapping the remainder of her dinner, a half-eaten slice of lasagna, she set her plate in the sink and grabbed her freshly printed resume off the counter. She went into the living room. Grandma Faith was sitting quietly in her rocking chair, knitting. She glanced up as she entered. "Don't you need to leave?"

"Yes, I'm trying to hurry. I need to drop this resume off at *Petco* to the hiring manager and then I'm going."

"Wait one minute." Setting her knitting needles and yarn down beside her chair, Grandma Faith rose to her feet and went into the kitchen. Returning with a plate of chocolate chip cookies with a foil cover, she handed them to Kylie. "Give them to that gentleman at *Petco*. It'll leave a good impression."

"Thank you."

"You're welcome, dear. Now run along."

Kylie went back into the bedroom she shared with her two-year-old son Peter and kissed his forehead. He was asleep. "Do well for Grandma, little man."

Taking her purse and coat off the rack near the front door, Kylie lifted a prayer of thankfulness to God and left.

Grandma Faith had been sweet enough to let her move in two years ago after the friend she was living with suddenly passed away. Kylie had made mistakes, but Grandma Faith loved her regardless of them. That woman's love was a constant reminder to Kylie of how much God loved her, despite her imperfections.

CHAPTER 6

KYLIE - AGE 7

*W*HEN KYLIE'S FEAR-LIT EYES landed on Grandma Faith for the first time, she turned in the doorway and sprinted to the car that had brought her. She didn't want to live with a stranger. She wanted to go back home to be with her mom. She wanted to go back to their little apartment on Ash Street where she had friends like Neese and Kanya to play with and her mom there with her most evenings. Kylie didn't want a new life.

The social worker pried Kylie's fingers off the door handle of the car and brought her kicking and screaming back to the house. Once inside, the social worker told her to sit on the couch and spoke with Grandma Faith in the kitchen. Kylie, arms crossed and heart full of anger, didn't move from the couch cushion she was placed on. When one of the other girls tried to invite her to play with dolls, she refused.

"I don't play with dolls. They're not real."

The little girl walked away with glistening tears in her eyes and a broken heart. Kylie turned her body away from the other kids in the room and looked at the TV that was turned off. She remembered her mom. Just a few days ago, they were watching SpongeBob and laughing together. Now everything was different. Everything was wrong. *How long do I have to be here?* She wondered. How long until her mom would come find her and rescue her from this unknown place? Would her mother even be able to find her if she tried? The lack of the possibility terrified her little heart.

After the social worker left, Grandma Faith came into the living room.

"Family meeting. Go tell the others." She smoothed a hand over one of the little girl's heads. The young gal scurried off to tell the others, while the kids still in the room took seats on the couches. There were three kids in the room, not including Kylie. All the children soon filled the room.

Grandma Faith came and sat down beside Kylie, but it caused Kylie to turn away more. She placed a hand on Kylie's shoulder.

"I know you're scared, but you don't have to be scared anymore. You're home now."

Whipping around, Kylie sat up. "This isn't my home! My mom is going to come get me and she'll take me *home*."

"Okay. Well, until that happens, how about you try to make the best of it? Maybe think of it as a sleepover."

"A sleepover with strangers? No, thanks."

"We don't have to be strangers, Kylie. We're all friends here."

Kylie glanced at the other children. There were nine girls in total. Grandma Faith had everyone in the room introduce themselves to Kylie. When it came to Kylie's turn, she didn't speak.

"Oh, come on, Kylie." The girl that went by the name of Betty pushed her to speak. "Don't be a sissy baby. Introduce yourself."

"Now, now, Betty," Grandma Faith warned. "Show God's kindness."

"What's the point of sharing?" Kylie opened her arms up, glaring at each girl in the room, then at Grandma Faith. "I won't be here long. My mom is going to find me."

"Yeah, I thought that too." Betty shook her head. "The quicker you get to accepting reality, the quicker you can move on and face the sad music."

Grandma Faith cut Betty off. Touching Kylie's shoulder softly, her mouth curved into a smile. "If you don't want to share, that's fine. Maybe tomorrow, you will change your mind."

The family meeting moved forward without participation from Kylie. They discussed their latest adventures in the back yard which consisted of a tree house and a full-sized playground. They also talked about a gentleman by the name of Albert who came weekly and taught the children about God, manners, and life. All the children appeared to be okay with their living arrangements at Grandma Faith's house, but Kylie wasn't going to be one of them. She'd have her mom back soon, and things would go back to normal. The Faith House was just a temporary stop.

CHAPTER 7

*H*ANDING THE PROPOSAL TO TYLER, Jonathan turned to Rose in her high chair beside him and gave her another saltine cracker. She took it willingly. His brother kept quiet as he thumbed each page carefully. On the pages with the design sketches, he'd turn the booklet sideways, analyzing each drawing, studying it carefully. After he was finished, he tossed it back to Jonathan, letting it slide across the table and fall into his lap.

"I'm sorry, brother, but it's sub-par work. We've been working together for how long now?"

"You know how long."

"Yep, I do. And in all of our time working together, I've never seen anything so half-way done before in my life. What is wrong with you?"

The waiter came over to their table and refilled their glasses of water. As the waiter finished, he told Jonathan and Tyler he was about done with his shift and a new waitress would soon be taking over the table.

"Okay, thanks. You've been great." Jonathan reached into

his back pocket and pulled out a ten and handed it to him. He put his wallet away and the waiter left their table. Jonathan knew the work he had done was sub-par on his part. That's why he had spent the majority of last night trying to fix everything wrong with it, but even his last-minute changes weren't enough. He couldn't hide from the truth. Not with himself, and not with Tyler. He was treading water and barely keeping his head above the surface. He let out a heavy sigh and looked at his brother across the table. "I don't like blaming a child, but I know that's the difference in my life right now. I'm struggling to balance my work and taking care of her."

Tyler smiled at Rose for a moment, then looked back at Jonathan. "You have plenty of money. Hire someone to take care of her during the day."

He had already thought about that idea, even acted on it. He went as far as running an ad on Spokane's Craigslist for half a day. He ended up taking the ad down, though, after he received over twenty applicants in the matter of a couple of hours. "I did try that, put an ad out, but got way too many applicants rolling in. Do you know how long it'll take to interview each of those people? Read all their emails and also work and take care of Rose? That's without mentioning the fact that I wouldn't know who they were or anything and let them into my home for the interview." He shuddered at the thought. "I don't want a bunch of random people coming into my house."

A waitress came over to the table with Jonathan and Tyler's food. She was pretty and had curly dark brown hair pulled back into a nice ponytail. After setting the plates down, she bent down to eye level with Rose. "I'll be right back with your food, munchkin."

She asked if there was anything else the two of them needed.

Jonathan laughed. "Yes, one more thing. Can you watch her for me Monday through Friday?"

She blinked without speaking a word. Then after a moment passed, she spoke. "Are you serious?"

Tyler looked at Jonathan, Jonathan at Tyler. Then he turned to her. "Maybe . . . ?" He lowered his voice and leaned toward her while she leaned toward him. "Are you looking to leave your job here?"

"Yes, as a matter of fact, I am. I just took a plate of cookies and a resume to *Petco.*"

"Hmm. Can I have a plate of cookies?" Jonathan tipped a smile. "I'm just playing. Do you have any experience with children?"

"I have a two-year-old son, and I helped a lot with my sisters when I was growing up."

Jonathan fished a business card from his pocket. "You're hired. Come to my house on Monday morning at seven o'clock and we'll get you started."

"What?"

"I said come to my house on Monday. The address is on the card."

She appeared confused. "Um . . . what's the pay?"

"Whatever you make here, doubled. You'll have evenings and weekends off."

Kylie's eyes began to water. "Wow, Mr." —she peered at the card— "Dunken. You are an answer to my prayers."

Jonathan's heart jolted at her mention of 'prayer.' He hadn't done much praying since Marie. Disregarding it and embracing the fact that he had just hired a nanny, he smiled. "Sure. See you Monday."

As she walked away from the table, Tyler's mouth gaped open. "You sly guy. You just snagged yourself a solution to your problem in just a couple of minutes."

"Maybe now I'll be able to get some work done." Jonathan

picked up his glass of water and took a long drink as he glanced in Kylie's direction.

CHAPTER 8

YLIE MET WITH HER FRIEND Savannah the following Sunday after services at their favorite little sandwich shop on the north side of Spokane. The May sun was warm, but not hot, so the two of them chose a table out on the balcony. Savannah was one of the ladies from the Bible study she had started going to on Tuesday nights. Kylie brought Peter along to their lunch date.

As the waitress took the menus, Kylie brushed her hand over the top of Peter's head as he sat in his high chair. She loved being near him any chance she had. There wasn't a lot of time left in the week after her work and online college coursework.

When the waitress had left their table, Kylie turned to her friend. "I got a job. I start tomorrow."

Savannah's face lit up, delighted to hear the wonderful news since Kylie had been struggling at *Ethan's* for months. She knew all about how often she was stuck late into the night, missing out on time with Peter.

"Do tell. Where?" Savannah asked, then her shoulders sagged as something seemed to come to her mind. "Please tell me it's not at that horrible gift shop in the mall you applied to a few months ago."

"Actually, it's not. It's kind of random how I got it. I'm going to be babysitting for a guy."

"For a guy?" Her friend's guard and eyebrows went up. "What *guy*?"

Kylie grabbed Jonathan's business card from her purse and handed it to her. "He's an architect and seemed really nice at the restaurant."

"At the restaurant? You mean you met him at *Ethan's*?"

"Yep."

Savannah adjusted in her seat, crossing her arms. "You're serious about this? Someone at one of your tables offered you a job and you just accepted on the spot? Did you already quit *Ethan's* and are just hoping it doesn't turn into a bad joke?"

Kylie shook her head. "Don't worry, Savannah. I'll quit once I make sure tomorrow that everything is legit. Frankly, I'm not too worried about it though. People aren't as shady as you think they are. He had his daughter with him. Pretty cute."

"The kid or him?" Savannah's head was tilted, a smile curling on her lips. "Please tell me this guy is not attractive, dear. Just please tell me this at least."

A blush crawled up Kylie's neck and into her cheeks. She found Mr. Dunken very attractive at the restaurant, but she hadn't thought that influenced her decision . . . or had it? She started to question herself. She steered the conversation toward the little girl. "His daughter was darling."

Savannah said, "And he was . . . ?"

Kylie studied her friend's face as she eagerly awaited a response. "He was attractive, but this is business. Plus, the guy is probably married."

Savannah shook her head. "Girl, don't be dumb. You can't

honestly think he's married *and* he needs someone to watch his daughter?"

"I'll be *fine*. I promise." Kylie held her eye contact with her friend. "Believe it or not, I can make good choices in life. Plus, he lives really close to Grandma Faith's house, so I get more time with Peter since I have a shorter commute and don't have to work nights. This is a God thing. Trust me."

After the meal, when it was time to leave, Savannah lingered at the table as Kylie loosened Peter from his high chair. Savannah touched Kylie's arm gently and looked at Peter, then at her. "Know that I love you and don't want you to get hurt again."

"Thank you. I appreciate your friendship and concern for me." Standing up with Peter in her arms, she looked at her little guy. "I know God will lead me and help me. I just have to keep trusting and walking in His will and His Spirit."

JONATHAN TURNED around from leaning into the back seat of his Camaro to find Rose had vanished. Worry flickered in his heart as his eyes darted all around him. He had only spent a minute trying to figure out how to tighten the straps on her five-point harness car seat and that appeared to be just enough time for her to escape. His heart pounded.

"Rose!" His voice got louder as he continued calling out to her. Seconds piled on one another and his forehead began to perspire.

Stepping out onto the sidewalk, he spotted her little red dress a block away. Relief came over him. Sprinting down the sidewalk, he quickly made his way down to the yard she was in, and as he approached, a woman came into view on her knees in front of a garden bed.

"Hey. Sorry, I turned my back for a second and she was gone."

The woman turned on her knees and he recognized her eyes under the brim of her dark brown sun hat. It was the woman from the restaurant, the one he had hired. "Kylie?"

"Yes?" She paused, squinting as she held up a gloved hand, peering at him. "Oh, Mr. Dunken! I knew you lived around here because of your card. I just didn't think we'd see each other so soon."

"Wow, it's a small world. Call me Jonathan, please. You live here?"

"Yes, I do. With my grandmother. You know, I thought I recognized her when she came up to me. By the way, what's this girl's name? You never told me at *Ethan's*."

"Rose. It's her mother's favorite flower."

"Mrs. Dunken must be a lucky lady." Jonathan heard the comment but was too stricken by a slice of pain rippling through him at the mention of Mrs. Dunken that he didn't respond to it. Then Kylie took off her gardening gloves and set them to the side. Then she picked a ladybug off from the collar of Rose's dress and set it on her own index finger. Holding her finger up a few inches from Rose's eyes, she whispered softly. "Be gentle with God's creation."

Wide-eyed and eager to touch it, Rose delicately brought her little fingers up and brushed the back of the ladybug. "Pretty."

Jonathan peered over into the grass and saw a bag of fertilizer and some garden tools. "You like to garden?"

She put the ladybug into Rose's hands and stood up. Brushing her hands off on her jeans, she shook her head. "Not really. I do it for my grandma. She's getting older and can't do as much as she'd like to do."

"That's nice of you. Hey, we were just going to head to the

park. Did you want to come with us? You can get to know the clientele."

"I have a sleeping kiddo inside myself, or I'd say yes for sure."

"Oh, that's too bad about the sleeping kid. Maybe next time!"

Taking Rose by the hand, he told her to say goodbye to Kylie. She waved.

"See you tomorrow."

"Absolutely. Looking forward to it."

Walking back to his driveway, he glanced over his shoulder at Kylie down the block. It seemed that even if he hadn't met her at the restaurant, they would've met regardless when he lost Rose. It made him think of his old faith in God he had left behind after losing Marie four years ago. He knew exactly what he'd say about the coincidences going on all around him. He'd say something about how God was helping him with Rose. How God had orchestrated it. Though he had faded from his faith, he still had it and thought about it from time to time. The difference between that time before Marie passed and now was that the power had gone from his faith. Now it was but a shadow of something that once was and is no longer, just like his wife.

CHAPTER 9

*M*ONDAY MORNING AT SEVEN O'CLOCK, Kylie gave Mr. Dunken's large oversized oak door a few solid knocks, then stepped back and waited. She had struggled that morning on whether she should dress comfortably in a pair of jeans and a t-shirt or in a dress, but she ended up settling on something in between. A nice pair of well-ironed gray slacks and a semi-fancy blouse. The outfit gave her a sense of style but was also comfortable. She knew she'd be chasing a two year old as her primary job, and that meant she needed clothing that allowed for flexibility.

When there was no answer after a few minutes, she decided to ring the doorbell. Soon enough, the door opened.

With a towel around his neck, a layer of sweat on his sculpted body, and only a pair of gym shorts on, Jonathan didn't make her feel very comfortable.

A blush climbed up her neck and into her cheeks at his appearance. She shielded her eyes and turned around. "Didn't you say seven?"

"Yes, sorry. I lost track of time on the treadmill. Turn around and come on in." Jonathan held the door open as he patted his face with the towel. "I'll go take a quick shower and meet you in a short while. Go ahead and go hang out with Rose. I just put her in the living room with some toys."

Still guarding her eyes, Kylie crossed the threshold into the house. Keeping her eyes on the floor and not on his impeccable physique, she walked through the foyer and into the living room. As her eyes fell on Rose, she smiled and felt the awkwardness between her and Jonathan melt away. Removing her hands from her face, she approached Rose and knelt to greet her.

AFTER SHOWERING, Jonathan put on a pair of jeans and a white button-up shirt. His hair was still wet and a few of the top buttons of his shirt were undone when he finally came downstairs. Finding Rose with a smile and enjoying her time with Kylie, Jonathan was relieved. He already felt the arrangement working marvelously for all three of them. She joined him in the kitchen, and they went over the employment paperwork she had to fill out to get paid.

"What exactly does my job entail?"

"That's a fair question. Um, I just need your help. You're basically here to help make my life easier."

"So, taking care of Rose. Doing some laundry? Shopping?"

"Sure." He laughed as he caught sight of the pile of laundry sitting randomly on the table in his kitchen. Pointing it out, he looked at Kylie. "I was going to get to that today. I swear."

Her smile was pleasant as it broke across her lips. It made him feel easy, relaxed. Raising her hands up, she shook her head. "I'm not here to judge. Just here to help. I'll take care of that and anything else around the house you need done for what you're paying."

"Sounds good to me. I appreciate your taking this on and giving it a chance. I know it was odd how it happened."

She tilted her head, still smiling. "Yes, a tad unconventional, but then again, a lot of what God does is that way."

Her mention of God was the third time in a row, making a mention of Him once every time they were together. The mention at the restaurant about answered prayers, the mention of God's creation to Rose, and now this. "You value your faith a lot, don't you, Kylie?"

He picked up an apple from the counter and bit into it.

"Well, of course, Mr. Dunken."

Waving his hand as he finished chewing, he shook his head. "I already told you yesterday to call me Jonathan."

"Okay, Jonathan. Yes, my faith is my strength and it comes with me everywhere I go. Is that going to be an issue with you?"

He wanted to say 'yes,' but that small voice in the depths of him knew he couldn't truthfully tell her that. "No, that's not a problem. Just curious."

Glancing at his watch, he held out his hands. "I guess I'd better get to work."

"That is why I'm here, *Jonathan*." She left the kitchen back to where Rose was in the living room. Smiling as a sense of freedom filled him, Jonathan headed to his studio to work on the redrafting of the designs for the project proposal.

CHAPTER 10

KYLIE - AGE 12

*K*YLIE HAD POSITIONED HER BED NEAR the window in her shared room with Jenny at Grandma Faith's on purpose when she first came to live there five years ago. She'd spend the evenings, after lights out, sitting on her bed and staring out into the moonlit night, waiting for Mama to come find her. She didn't pray to God but instead to her mother, hoping she'd be able to hear her somehow. Her roommate, Jenny, knew of her nightly prayers and tried a few times to tell her about a friend of hers she prayed to named Jesus. Kylie shut her down every time, just like she did with Grandma Faith.

One night, while her head lay pressed against the glass of her window, she was about asleep when Jenny sat up.

"It's been five years, Kylie. Isn't it about time you face reality?"

Blinking her eyes to fight away the tears, Kylie lifted her head from the glass pane. She turned to Jenny. "I don't know how to let go."

"Just give it to Jesus. He will take it for you."

Kylie didn't like it when Jenny or anyone at The Faith

House tried to talk to her about this Jesus fellow. It was always 'Jesus this and Jesus that.' They spoke of a man as some sort of magical genie, and she just couldn't buy into the concept of a Savior. The only man she ever knew left her and Mama when she was just a toddler. "Tell me this, Jenny. If this Jesus guy is so great, why'd He ever let my mom get rid of me? Why'd He allow for your parents to get rid of you?" Her eyes turned back to the window. Peering down at the street light on the corner of Emerson and Place Street, sadness invaded her heart. "Seems to be if there was some big loving God in the sky out there, He wouldn't allow for so much pain."

Jenny didn't speak again that night. Instead, she rolled over and prayed for Kylie. The entirety of The Faith House household prayed for Kylie. She needed the Lord's peace a lot more than she had realized. It had been hard for Kylie since coming to the house. Multiple times, she had attempted to leave. Luckily, everyone on the block had eyes on the lookout for kids running away from The Faith House. They'd phone Grandma Faith every time a child tried to run off, which happened more often since Kylie had arrived. Sometimes, it was Kylie running, and other times, it was other girls who wanted to run from Kylie.

As Kylie continued to look outside that evening, she knew in her heart that her hope was running dry on her mother. It had already been five years and not a peep from her.

A COUPLE OF WEEKS LATER, Grandma Faith asked Kylie to come join her for afternoon tea alone in the living room after her Bible lesson with Albert. The rest of the children were outside playing while they spent time one-on-one. These meetings might have been 'requests' by Grandma Faith, but every child in that house knew they weren't optional. Kylie plopped down on the couch while Grandma Faith was already sitting down in the recliner. At Kylie's arrival, Grandma Faith rose from her seat and poured cups of tea for the two of them.

"What do you want to talk about?" Kylie pressed, not wanting to spend too much time with the woman she held responsible for her misery.

"I wanted to ask if you'd be interested in my adopting you. As you know, it's been over five years now. You're also at the age where the judge will ask you if you desire to be adopted."

"No." Kylie jumped from the couch, her arms opening up. "You seriously think I'd want to be adopted by you?"

Grandma Faith's hands trembled as she sat down with her tea in the recliner. She didn't take a drink of her tea or speak a word in that moment. She merely listened.

"If you want to do something for me, you can find my mom and tell her where I am so I can get out of this prison." She started to cry as she flung her hands in the air. "I've been waiting and waiting for her and I know she's out there looking for me! She just doesn't know where I'm at!"

Setting her tea down on the end table beside her chair, Grandma Faith held a heavy frown in her expression. "My child. You have no idea, do you? I figured with the internet in the recreation room, you would've found out by now."

"Found out what?" Kylie wiped her eyes, eager to learn even a shred about her mother. When a moment passed and Grandma Faith still hadn't spoken, Kylie pressed again, wanting to know.

"Your mother passed away, dear. It was shortly after you arrived here. I'm sorry. I thought you knew."

The breath in her lungs pressed out, and Kylie sat down on the couch in the living room. Numb inside, burning tears filled her eyes. "How is that possible?" Touching her chest with a trembling hand, she continued. "Why couldn't I feel that all this time? I should've been able to know she was gone."

Compassion lifted Grandma Faith up from her seat and brought over to the couch beside Kylie. Wrapping an arm around her, she brought Kylie in close. "I'm so sorry you didn't know." She kissed the top of Kylie's head and rubbed her back in a circular motion. "This is your family now. Betty, Jenny, Clair, Mary, and Albert. They are your family, and we all love each other."

"Yeah, but who knows how long those kids will be here? They can be here today and gone tomorrow like the others who were here when I first came. You love to tell us how you offer structure and balance and consistency, but then you have kids coming and going."

Grandma Faith didn't say anything in response for a long time. Then, she finally did say something. "I wasn't sure if you're old enough to know this, but I think you are. I am working on closing down the foster care aspect of the house. It's already in the process. My plan is to adopt all of you as soon as I can. You'll be the first one, Kylie. If you allow it."

Still distraught over losing her mother, she couldn't agree to it, not now. "I'll think about it. Right now, I need to learn more about my mom." Rising to her feet, Kylie went into the recreation room of the house and got on the family computer. She needed to know what happened, no matter how painful it might be. She had to know what her mother's untimely death entailed, even if it was horrific. Was she a drug addict? Maybe she was a really bad person and that's why Kylie felt angry all the time? Maybe it was just part of her DNA?

A soft hand touched her shoulder before she started. It was Grandma Faith.

"My child, once you go down the path, there's no coming back from it. It'll change your thinking of her, warp your mind."

Kylie thought for a moment of her father. He had left her and her mother when she was only two, headed for Memphis, Tennessee to become a rock star. He was never heard from again. "I know. But I *need* to know who my mother truly was, good or bad." Turning back to the computer, she clicked the mouse on the screen.

CHAPTER 11

SKETCHING IN HIS STUDIO THE next morning, Jonathan's hand cramped and he set his pencil into the cup on his design table. Standing up, he clasped his hands together behind his back and stretched. Kylie soon entered the studio with a cup of steaming black coffee and a newspaper in hand.

"Thank you." Jonathan studied her as she crossed the smooth floor and over to the counter that lined the wall and was near to where he was standing. She set the cup down, then the newspaper. She looked pretty today. A nice dark blue dress, her hair pulled up, but a few strands down. She was a bit more relaxed than she was yesterday. Maybe it had something to do with the fact that he hadn't answered the door sweating like an animal and half-undressed. Regardless of the reason, he was glad.

"You don't see that a lot anymore, do you?" Jonathan's eyes lingered on hers as she met his gaze.

"What?" She blinked, a look of uncertainty flickering in her eyes. He approached her, then reached for the paper.

Grabbing it and the coffee, he walked back over toward his design table.

"The newspaper. People don't read anymore these days." He set his coffee down on the design table, then opened the paper, flipping to the business section. He grabbed his cup of coffee and took a deep drink, letting the hot liquid slightly burn as it traveled down his throat. She walked over to him.

"I thought the same thing when I saw it on your porch this morning. Newspapers in themselves are a dying breed from a different generation."

"You're right. I'm still subscribed because I love the way it smells. Honestly, the smell of anything in print is delightfully appealing to me. I also enjoy the feeling of turning a page in the newspaper or in a book. You can't get that flicking a screen."

"That's true. By the way, when Rose woke up this morning and I retrieved her from her bed, she had a stuffy nose. I couldn't find anything in the cupboards in the kitchen. Where do you keep your medicine?"

Folding the paper, he set it down on the table. "The medicine cabinet in the bathroom in my bedroom has all my medicine, but I don't have anything for children. You'll need to go to the store for that." Jonathan pulled out his wallet and handed her a credit card. "Grab some food while you're out also. I know there isn't much."

"Okay." The card slipped out of her hand and she bent at the knees to grab it off the floor. As she did, Jonathan noticed the top of a tattoo on her neck. The collar of her dress hid most of it, but he saw enough to know there was more to her than just the God façade she'd been putting off since they met. Curiosity piqued in him as she stood back upright. "I'm sorry. My fingers are a little clumsy at times."

"It's okay. Tell me, *Kylie*. What is your biggest regret in life?"

"A bit personal, don't you think?"

Jonathan raised his hands. "My apologies."

"It's okay. I am curious about something about you."

"Please ask."

"You don't have medicine for your child and you suddenly are in need of someone to watch Rose. I feel like I'm . . ."

"Missing something?" Jonathan finished her sentence, tipping a smile as he did. He raised a hand. "I should have explained things more to you. Rose is my niece. My sister-in-law showed up a while back and left her child with me. I've been doing what I can to take care of her, but with my work, it's just too much."

"Oh, I see."

Sensing her uneasiness, Jonathan raised his eyebrows. "My work is demanding and I don't see the situation with Rose's mom changing anytime soon. Don't worry about anything. I have temporary guardianship of Rose right now, and I have a court date in two months for permanent guardianship."

She hesitated to respond. He sensed it.

"What? Go ahead. You don't need to be shy with me, Kylie."

"And Mrs. Dunken?"

He didn't expect her to go there, though it made sense for her to ask. Jonathan could have been tipped over with a feather at the mention of Marie. Jonathan's spirit felt jolted and jumbled around like a pair of Yahtzee dice. "Why would you ask about a Mrs. Dunken?"

Her cheeks went crimson. "Sorry. I mentioned a Mrs. Dunken on Sunday and you didn't say anything, I figured then there wasn't one, but I saw on your mantle a wedding photo and—"

He held up a hand. Jonathan wanted her to stop talking

about her, to stop mentioning her in the conversation. It only drove the dagger deeper into his heart. He had spent the last three years trying to feel okay enough to get through a day without tears. He didn't need someone stirring the cauldron of pain. "There is no Mrs. Dunken anymore. Let's leave it at that and not talk about her again, please."

Awkwardness soon invaded the quiet between them, but Kylie moved. She lifted a drawing from his table and looked it over. He glanced to see which one it was. It was a structure that he had designed for a ritzy single Malibu schmuck who wanted modern and chic. She studied it carefully and then set it back down without a word.

"What do you think of it?" He wanted to hear how she viewed his work.

"Seems a bit much. The curves along the whole right side? Wavy? Like, seriously?"

Jonathan laughed, crossing his arms and covering part of his mouth. "I know. The guy who requested the design is a bit much himself."

"Oh, so the design fits the gentleman."

They both laughed.

She was about to leave when she turned to Jonathan and peered into his eyes. "By the way, Jonathan. You're doing the right thing by taking Rose in and raising her. No matter how long that ends up being. I just wanted you to know that."

"Thanks."

She left his studio and he returned to work. As he sketched, he felt distracted. He couldn't think clearly. Marie had danced across his thoughts and rested on his mind. Crinkling the paper, he tossed it into the garbage can. Then he started sketching what came to mind—the tattoo on Kylie. It had only been a small portion he had seen on the back of her neck, but it had intrigued him. When he finished the drawing, he set his pencil down, then picked up the paper. He turned it and studied the odd shape. It had words, but he didn't get a good enough mental image to know what it said, and then a pattern that reminded him of something Irish. Setting the paper back down, he pulled out his colored pencils and filled in the colors. Shaded with dark blue, outlined purple. Setting his colored pencils back into their drawer, he leaned back in his chair and studied the image. Letting his mind concentrate more on the design, questions surfaced. Was it just a small design on her neck? Or did the tattoo spread over the entirety of Kylie's neck and onto her back? Regardless of its size and purpose, it told Jonathan one thing. Kylie had a past too.

A FEW DAYS LATER, Kylie got a call from Savannah. She wanted to catch up over coffee and learn about how the new job was going. They met at a coffee shop near Savannah's apartment complex on Francis Street in Spokane. After getting their coffees, they sat down at a table inside the shop. Peter didn't come along for the trip. He was already asleep in his bed by the time she left the house.

"So, is he married?"

"No, but he was at some point."

Savannah must've noticed something in Kylie's face at that point. "Was he rude about it or something?"

"Kind of, but not really. I don't know. He just didn't want to discuss it."

"She's either dead or she cheated on him. Mmmhmm. He's damaged goods, honey. Run."

Kylie shook her friend's notion out of her head. "I'm working for him, not dating him."

"You keep it that way. A man like that never changes without the power of God. Is he a Christian?"

"It's hard to say. He doesn't curse or anything like that, but he gets quiet anytime I mention my faith."

"And you do that a lot, so I'm sure he's somewhere between believer and doubter. You toss in a cheating spouse or a dead one, and you've got yourself a mental basket case for a man."

"Well, like I said, good thing I'm not dating him. Right?"

"Yes."

For the next hour, Savannah started telling Kylie about a new guy she had met at the coffee shop earlier that week. She was crushing on the guy after one date, talking about how they were going to get married, he was going to give her beautiful babies, and how she planned to get a dog after they got settled into their new house after marriage. Savannah had high hopes and a good heart with every man she dated, but she moved too quickly for all of them and they ended up running by the third or fourth encounter with the lady.

"Going back to this Jonathan fellow. You're not attracted to him. Correct?"

"I'd be lying if I didn't say he's attractive."

Savannah leaned across the table. "You're a good person, but you trust your heart out to people too easily. Be careful."

After their coffee and Kylie's drive home, she asked God for help. *Please, God. Lead me in the way I should go. If this man is too much of a temptation for me, let me know somehow. I want to serve You, Lord. I want to care for my sweet little man, but I don't need more of what You don't will in my life.*

Pulling into the driveway, she shut off her car. She felt a peace fall over her anxious thoughts. Kylie knew right then that the job was right for her at the current time. As she got ready for bed that night, she got a text from Savannah.

You should start coming to Christian Singles Night at the

church. It's on Sunday evenings from 6-9. Usually, there are snacks and a fun little activity. I barely ever meet anyone there, but it's worth a shot. Right?

You're right. I'll try it out. It can't hurt to meet Christian men.

$\mathcal{W}$AKING ON THE MORNING OF Rose's permanent guardianship hearing two months later, Jonathan smelled something he hadn't in a long time—bacon. The aroma brought him out of his slumber with a smile on his face. Pushing off his comforter and sheets, he left his room. Skipping his morning workout, he hurried his steps through the hallway and down the stairs in pursuit of the delicious smell. Venturing into the kitchen, he found Kylie at the stove and Rose in the high chair a few feet from her.

"What did I do in order to be spoiled with a home-cooked breakfast?" Jonathan flashed a questioning gaze with a soft smile toward Kylie on his way to the cupboard.

"I know you've been a little stressed about the big court day being today. Figured a nice breakfast might set you at ease. After all, you hired me to make your life easier, did you not?" Kylie moved from the stovetop over to the counter and flopped a pair of cooked eggs onto a plate.

"Well, thank you." Pulling down a coffee cup from the

cupboard, he poured a cup of coffee. He took a sip, studying Kylie as she moved gracefully from Rose's high chair and back over to the stove. He admired the way she moved. It wasn't the usual forced and stressed way he seemed to do everything in life. He was always needing to get back to work in his studio. Jonathan barely had enough time to pour a cup of coffee without spilling it on the counter, let alone move through the kitchen like she did, gracefully and with a sense of purpose.

Her mouth tipped a smile as she looked over and met his gaze from the stove as he sat down. He smiled back at her. When she finally made her way over and sat with him, there was a certain feeling of rightness with it. Jonathan was getting comfortable with the three of them together and their routine.

Kylie reached out to the side and pulled Rose's high chair closer to the table. Rose giggled as the high chair vibrated across the tile floor.

As Jonathan ate his food, he studied Kylie, watching her as she fed Rose, and looked at the comic section of the newspaper. He felt an inclination to learn more about the woman. Maybe it was the bacon that had prompted the idea, or maybe it was just the fact that she showed him kindness. Whatever the reason was, he knew he wanted to know more. "I don't know much about you. I do know you have a son named Peter. How old is he?"

"He is two."

"You married?"

"I was."

"That's a rather short answer." Just then, he recalled not sharing about Marie when she had inquired about a Mrs. Dunken in his life. He didn't want to share then, and he didn't want to share now. Jonathan shifted topics quickly. "Which is fine. What else is going on with you? Do you plan to nanny forever or do you have other aspirations?" Jonathan took a bite of his toast.

Raising her eyebrows, her eyes widened and a joy lit up in them as something surfaced to her mind. "I'm taking a few online college courses to get my degree in Early Childhood Education. My passion is children."

Jonathan raised an eyebrow, glancing at Rose for a moment, then back at her. "That explains why you're so good with children. I really got lucky when you ended up taking my table at *Ethan's*."

"God is good all the time. Always working, never sleeping."

Jonathan swallowed the uncomfortable lump in his throat. He slipped under his breath as he brought the fork with egg on it up to his lips, "Don't give *Him* the credit."

"Why not give Him credit?"

He knew what she was doing by asking *why*. She was leading him, trying to unravel his personal history. Jonathan could've gotten up and left the kitchen at that particular moment, but he did not. He stayed. Taking a drink of his coffee, he chose his words carefully. "Kylie. With all due respect, it's a coincidence that you were there and I was there. You simply desired a new job and I had one for you." Jonathan shrugged. "Just a chance meeting."

"Who are you trying to convince? I've seen you these last two months. Every time I even hint at faith or God, you recoil and remove yourself from the conversation or steer it elsewhere."

"Yeah? I don't like talking about God. Faith is a crutch for the weak-minded."

"But you believe, Jonathan. I see it in your face every time I mention Jesus's name. Sure, there's pain mingled in there, but you know that name."

His soul stirred, just like it did every time he heard the

name of Jesus. It wasn't by choice, for his heart and emotions were deadened by years of running. He didn't respond to her comment but just focused on his meal before him. He didn't want to keep talking about God, talking about Jesus, or anything else. He just wanted to eat.

A blush settled into her cheeks. His silence must've unnerved her. She reached over beside her chair and pulled from her tote bag a few children's books. She laid them across the table. "Now that we're on the topic, I've been meaning to talk to you. These are faith-inspired Children's books. I didn't want to overstep my bounds by assuming they're okay. If they're not, I'll put them back in my bag and leave them at home."

Standing up, Jonathan peered over at Rose. His heart loved her, cared for her, wanted what was best. Deep down, he knew it was right for her to have a knowledge of God, a knowledge of His creation. "Yes, those are fine for Rose."

Finished, he took his plate to the sink. As he set it down, Kylie caught his ear. "Can I still mention God? Or would that be too offensive to you?"

Jonathan couldn't forbid it. "It's okay to mention God whenever you feel moved to. Just don't expect me to care or engage. I have to go get ready for court now. Thanks again for breakfast."

"Okay. By the way, Tyler called. He said he'll meet you at the courthouse a few minutes to ten. Also, I'm going to take Rose down the block to have lunch with my Grandma around noon."

"Sounds good. Thanks for letting me know about Tyler."

Leaving the kitchen, Jonathan headed upstairs to shower and get dressed for his day in court. He had a sneaking suspicion that Rose's mother, Shawna, might try to show up in court and fight for custody. The CPS lawyer assured him that there was nothing that she could do at this point, but that did little to ease the worry pressing against his thoughts and mind. He had barely slept the last week leading up to this day. He was ready for his day in court to be over before it had even begun.

CHAPTER 13

*T*HE COURT DATE WAS SET for Kylie's adoption by Grandma Faith. Kylie had lost hours, days, weeks, and months of sleep in anticipation. A part of her prayed her mother would show up and fight for her, but in her heart, she knew it wasn't possible. Her mother had been dead from an overdose for six years. She had died from Meth, or as Grandma Faith called it, *the devil's vomit*. The day she had looked up her mother's name on the computer, she read an article from the local news detailing her mother's untimely end. She didn't cry but felt numb all over for the first couple of days. Then she cried a sad cry as she mourned the loss of her mother. She couldn't understand why her mother would do it, how she could pick drugs over her, but the cold reality was that she had.

In the courtroom, with all her grief and emotions running high within her heart, Kylie's eyes glistened as the judge granted adoption to Grandma Faith. She didn't like Grandma Faith much, but she was starting to appreciate the fact that she had taken her in. She wouldn't have ever met Betty, her now best friend, who had also lost her mother to drugs. They spent hours beneath the jungle gym, sharing in one another's pain. Betty understood her hurt more than anyone else at The Faith House, or at least that's how Kylie felt.

After court, all the girls from The Faith House went out to eat, an occasion that rarely happened in the household. Kylie got to pick the place to eat, so she picked her favorite place in the world to go, *Old Country Buffet*. She wasn't a big eater, but she did love the endless glasses of chocolate milk that were at her disposal when they went there. Grandma Faith let the girls eat and drink whatever they wanted when they went to a buffet. She found it easier that way than trying to micromanage all eight of the girls at one time.

Sitting at the table while all the other kids were already gone at the buffet, Kylie's head rested on the palm of her hand as she held a sad frown. Grandma Faith noticed her and came over to sit next to Kylie. "My child, today is a good day. What is wrong?"

A sad smile on Kylie's lips told Grandma Faith everything she needed to know.

Resting a hand on her back, she leaned slightly toward Kylie. "I know you miss your mom, and I'll never be what you had with her. I don't expect to be. But I will tell you one thing, child. I'm adopted too."

Kylie's interest was piqued, and she lifted her head up and turned to her. "You are?"

"Yes. I've been grafted into the family of God. All Christians are adopted by God into His family. That's the beautiful thing about God, about adoption. Adoption means someone *chose* you. Just like God chose to adopt us, I chose to adopt you, Kylie. Do you understand?"

"Yes." Kylie's whole body tingled as her heart grabbed hold of God. This was the first time in her life that she had an interest in God. More so than any of the Bible verses and

Bible stories or any of the Sunday school classes she was forced to attend. Being adopted into the family of God meant something to her in a big way. Kylie's eyes turned to her fellow sisters in The Faith House as they piled food onto their plates. Then her gaze turned back to Grandma Faith. "So we're all part of God's family?"

"When you accept Jesus as your Lord and Savior over your life, yes, you're adopted into the family of God. Jesus is the Son of God. He makes it possible for us to enter into the family. My child, you see this world all around you? It's fading away, it's running down. What you see before you will be here today and gone tomorrow, but God's kingdom goes on forever. Our families here on earth are only temporary. The family of God goes on forever into eternity."

Kylie had been listening to the Bible and Grandma Faith for years, but now it was making sense, starting to draw her in. Her heart pounded. "Grandma Faith?"

"Yes, child?"

"I want to make Jesus my Lord and Savior. I know the Scriptures and I know the story of Christ dying on the cross, and I've believed it, but I didn't want to commit and surrender until now. I know now that I need Him. I desire to be a part of the family of God. I might not know my earthly father and I might have lost my earthly mother, but I know God is my true and heavenly Father."

She threw up her hands and lifted her voice. "Oh, praise the Lord! Let's pray."

That day marked two important events in Kylie's life. Not only had she been adopted into Grandma Faith's family, but also into the family of God. In what she felt would be the worst day of her life, she found peace. In the chaos of the storm, she felt the calling of God on her life. She wouldn't live a perfect life moving forward, but she'd have Jesus by her side from here to eternity.

CHAPTER 14

$\mathcal{C}$ARRYING HER PLATE WITH A peanut butter
sandwich on it, Kylie gently touched Grandma
Faith's shoulder as she slept in her rocking chair. If it wasn't
for the constricting and restricting of her chest, Kylie
would've sworn she had passed on to glory. Grandma Faith
had been given only a limited time left on this earth after the
cancer came back a month ago. The doctors and hospice told
her it's a matter of weeks, possibly months if she's lucky. It
tore Kylie apart inside to know the only woman to ever truly
be a mother to her would soon be gone from her life, but she
knew where she was heading, her new home in eternity.

"Thank you, my child." Grandma Faith lifted the sandwich with a trembling hand to her mouth and took a bite.
She set it back down on the plate and set the plate on the arm
rest. "These last couple of months have really shown me
what it means when the Scriptures say this body is wasting
away. I feel so tired all the time."

Kylie pushed a sad smile from her lips and rested a hand
on her arm. "I'm so sorry."

"It's going to be okay. Soon, I'll be with Jesus and I'll be dancing. Maybe even some of that break dancing."

Kylie's lips curled into a smile and she sat down on the couch. She pulled Rose from the floor and onto her lap. Jenny, Kylie's old roommate from The Faith House, walked in from the kitchen. She had moved back to the house when Grandma Faith found out about the cancer returning. She wanted to spend her final days with her, and thankfully, she was more than willing to help with Peter too.

"How was Jonathan this morning? Did he seem stressed?"

She shook her head, smoothing her hand over Rose's hair. "He seemed okay about that. How long ago did Peter go down for a nap?"

Jenny took a seat on the couch. Lifting her cell phone from the coffee table, she glanced at the time. "About fifty minutes ago. He woke up earlier than usual today and was tired or I would've kept him up for you."

Immediately, Kylie knew it wouldn't be until later that she'd see her little man. "Okay."

She glanced at her phone. It was twelve thirty now. She thought of Jonathan. She hoped everything was okay at court. The hearing had started over two hours ago now and she hadn't heard a word from him. Knowing that he had his brother with him brought a measure of comfort to her. Tyler was a good support system for him to lean on.

"You look worried." Grandma Faith's eyes might have been failing her, but her senses were in tip-top shape.

"I just haven't heard from Jonathan."

"Are you concerned for Jonathan or your boss?" Jenny implored. She had been suspicious of just how deep Kylie's feelings went for the man ever since she arrived back at The Faith House.

Kylie could feel her eyes studying her. "Both. I'm not interested in him in that way, if that's what you're asking. I know he's been stressing about court lately, and it's been affecting his sleep." Rising to her feet, she set Rose on her hip and grabbed the diaper bag from beside the couch. "I'm going to head back to the house. I love you both dearly. Thanks for all the help with Peter, Jenny. I don't know what I'd do without you here the last couple of months."

"It's my joy to serve you in this way while I'm here."

Leaning over, she kissed Grandma Faith's forehead and left.

On her walk back to Jonathan's driveway, she was stopped by two mothers with strollers.

"Cute girl. How old is she?"

"Two." Kylie turned around to greet the woman. She fell into a light conversation and through it found out that the two of them were from down the street and around the corner. They had the daily habit of walking the sidewalks and being a sort of 'neighborhood watch,' though it was unofficial. Kylie suspected they were just the type of women with a lot of time to stick their noses into other people's business.

"We should get our husbands together," one of the ladies said. "Our two husbands get along well. Sports, current events, politics."

"Oh, Jonathan and I aren't married. I'm just the nanny. He isn't into any of those kinds of things . . . at least I don't think."

"My apologies for assuming." Raising an eyebrow, the one woman who had been talking continued. "What do you mean he's not into those things? What else is there?"

"Art. Reading. He has a massive library in the back corner of his house."

The quiet one bit her lip as her eyes flashed with a look of lust. The other lady smacked her. "You're a married woman, Raine!"

"I'm sorry. I can't help but be fascinated by a man who can actually use that thing between the ears for something other than keeping batting records and yards gained in a season." Raine came closer to Kylie, lowering her voice as she raised an eyebrow. "Is he single?"

"Yes."

Raine slowly shook her head as she took a step backward. "Girl, you'd better nab that man before someone else does."

Just then, Jonathan honked, startling the two woman and forcing them to carry on their way down the sidewalk. A blush formed in Kylie's cheeks as she thought of the possibility of 'nabbing' him. He pulled into the driveway and she stepped into the grass. As the women went out of sight down the sidewalk, she directed her attention on Jonathan getting out of his car. She lifted Rose's hand up to wave to Jonathan.

He tipped a forced smile and headed for the front door without a word. Kylie could tell something was wrong.

SILENCE LINGERED in the air between Jonathan and Kylie over dinner. Jonathan couldn't shake what had happened in the courtroom. His mind was clouded. Sure, he had won and was awarded the guardianship over Rose, but at what cost? He relived the moment Shawna came storming into the courtroom with tears running down her cheeks. The screaming pierced through his thoughts as he tried to eat the roast Kylie had prepared.

"Jonathan?" Kylie's voice jolted him out of his thoughts. He blinked a few extra times then looked at her with a questioning gaze. "I asked you how court went. You've been silent all afternoon and over dinner. It's not like you to be *this* quiet."

He set his fork down and lifted his napkin from his lap. Bunching up the red-colored cloth, he tossed it on his half-eaten plate of food. "Shawna showed up and things were a bit . . . difficult. I'm going back to the studio. Everything okay here?"

"Yeah, but it's getting late. I need to get home. I'll be here for a half hour more, so until a quarter to six. That's the max I can do, Jonathan."

Her stern voice made it clear to him he'd better not try to fight it. "Fine. I'll be done in the studio by that time."

Leaving the dining room, Jonathan ventured up the glass stairs and down the quiet hallway to his studio. Getting inside, he shut the door behind him. He was back to where he felt comfortable, somewhere he could let loose. He was in his sanctuary.

Walking straight across the studio floor, he came to his design desk and kicked the stool out of the way. Grabbing a pencil from the cup, he began to sketch an outline of Shawna's face. The curves and base shapes first, then her eyes, then her hair, then the layers of details after that. The strand of hair that fell after she had attempted to tuck it all behind her ear. The burning tears as her mind and heart were confused over what was happening. He sketched quickly, leaving out no detail that was burned into his mind. Once done with the sketch, he pulled out colored pencils and brought life to it.

Jonathan set his final colored pencil down and stepped back as he lifted the drawing.

He knew he had done the right thing by taking guardianship over Rose. Everyone had done nothing but tell him it was right for the last two months. But it had still stung to see Shawna broken like she was in the courtroom. He'd never meant to hurt her. That wasn't what Marie would've wanted. He'd never meant for things to become ugly like they had.

But he couldn't endanger Rose to save Shawna's feelings. That wasn't right.

A gentle knock came a few moments later, then the door opened a fraction. Kylie peeked her head inside and Jonathan quickly set the drawing down on the table. He moved to block her view of the table as she approached.

"Yes?"

"I'm going."

"Oh, right. Let me walk you to the door." He met her halfway between the table and the door and walked with her, exiting and shutting the door behind him. As they walked together, he felt immensely better than he had all day. "I'm sorry about how I was earlier. Sometimes, I need time to process and think. Honestly, court went fine. Rose is under my care permanently now, and she'll be protected. What was a surprise today was Shawna showing up at the hearing."

"Oh, wow. They didn't expect that, right?"

"Right. She was a wreck. It was sad. You could tell she took the time to do her makeup and get all dressed up, but that wasn't enough to save her from herself in the courtroom. She ended up being kicked out by the judge because she couldn't control herself."

"That must've been hard to sit through." Kylie was soft in her words as they arrived to the front door in the foyer. She opened it. Turning back to Jonathan, she tilted her head slightly. "That little girl in there and I have some things in common, Jonathan."

Jonathan took a step closer. "What do you mean?"

"I was abandoned by my mother when I was seven." Her eyes glistened slightly, then she peered over his shoulder toward the other room where Rose was most likely playing with toys. "Rose is going to be okay. She will have questions, but she'll be okay. You're a good dad to her, and all that matters to a child is to have parents who care and are actually there for them."

He hadn't thought of himself once as a dad to Rose. He was Uncle Jonathan. His heart felt a flicker of warmth crash over it at her words of comfort and encouragement. "I had no idea you were abandoned as a child. I wouldn't have guessed that."

"There's a lot you don't know about me." She crossed the threshold of the doorway and stepped down the cement steps. Stopping, she glanced back at Jonathan. "Have a good night, Mr. Dunken."

Hearing her formality pushed him back into the right frame of mind. She was an employee and he was the employer.

CHAPTER 15

.

THAT EVENING, KYLIE FED PETER chicken, green beans, and applesauce shortly after six thirty. After clearing his tray, she lifted him from the high chair and held him close to her chest as she went to her bedroom. Lying on her bed atop the comforter, she brushed her fingers across the top of his head and sang him a lullaby. Her heart was a bit conflicted tonight and she held her son a little closer. She hadn't seen Jonathan emotionally conflicted before tonight, and it stirred something inside her. She had the sense there was a lot she didn't know about him, some good, some bad.

Kissing Peter's head as she finished the lullaby, she turned her gaze to the window. It was the same window she'd looked out as a child. The summer sun was still illuminating the sky outside at that time, and a small breeze was drifting in through the window's opening. Kylie still had homework for her college classes to do, but all she desired was to drift on to sleep with her son close to her.

Closing her eyes, she prayed. *God, I'm here and I'm willing to do whatever pleases You. This man, Jonathan, seems like trouble to me, and I'm not sure why I feel drawn to him. Help me know what Your will is in my life. Guide me, Lord. Please.*

Rising from her bed, she gently set her sleeping son down into his toddler bed and covered him with his *Cars* blanket. Tiptoeing over to her computer desk, she opened up her laptop. She had an email notification pop-up on her screen. It was from her friend, Savannah. Opening it, she read her email. It was lengthy, and that explained why she didn't text it. She detailed how this guy came into her work at *Macy's* and they got to talking and he mentioned he was a Christian. He's really into reading books and planned to take Savannah up on the offer to attend the singles' night thing at the church this coming Saturday evening.

Kylie rolled her eyes and let out a quiet laugh. She found it cute but humorous that her friend thought the guy was perfect because he shared an interest in reading. *There are plenty of men who enjoy reading . . . like Jonathan.* Realizing her thoughts were gravitating toward Jonathan, she felt moved to go meet this guy. Replying to her friend, she let her know she'd meet him. As she hit the *Send* button, she shook her head in humor at her friend's love for her.

Exiting the email, she opened up her classroom portal online and started her homework. As she worked on her assignments for her classes, a soft summer rain started outside, the sound drifting in from the open window.

AFTER PUTTING Rose to sleep for the evening, Jonathan still struggled with an icky feeling from court. He knew exactly what he needed—a good workout. After working up a sweat and a fast heartbeat on the treadmill, he peeled off his shirt and grabbed his towel. Hitting the weights next, he focused on pushing each fiber of his muscles to the max. After a solid hour, he took his already damp towel and traveled down the hallway toward his bedroom, patting the sweat off his face as he walked.

Upon entering his room, he turned on the lamp that sat on his dresser and went over to the double French doors leading out to the balcony. Unlatching the doors, he flung them open and a gust of cool summer air mingled with rain blew against his warm body, instantly cooling him off. His lips broke into a smile.

Wiping his chest off with the towel, he walked over and set it on his dresser. Opening one of the drawers that held his white folded T-shirts, he lifted the last one from the stack. There at the bottom was a drawing he had done months ago. It was the one he had sketched of Kylie's tattoo. Thinking about earlier and how she had mentioned there was more to her than he knew, he lifted the drawing with a heightened sense of curiosity as the two thoughts came together in his mind. She was right. There was more to her.

Inspecting the drawing, an old question he had asked himself when he originally drew it stirred. What was her story? He set the drawing down on top of the dresser and put on his shirt. As the shirt's fabric hugged against his skin, he felt his eyelids droop heavily. Jonathan was exhausted. Crossing his hardwood floor over to his bed, he let himself collapse fully onto the comforter. With the sound of the rain dancing against the wooden beams outside in the dark, he headed toward a sublime night of slumber. As he drifted further and further into sleep, Kylie's face pressed into his thoughts. What was her story?

CHAPTER 16

KYLIE - AGE 25

A GLASS VASE SLAMMED AGAINST the wall beside her, only inches from her cheek. Tremors were felt throughout her whole body as the evening's argument with her husband, Paul, had taken a turn for the worse. He had come home late from the office, and he had claimed on the telephone that he was working on a project, but Kylie flashed a questioning look about that fact when he came through the door smelling of cigars and booze. She didn't even say a word to him, but her glance toward him was enough to unhinge his evil side. The night started with light arguing, then, before she had time to even recognize the danger, he was chasing her through their house.

Holding up a hand as Paul charged across the bedroom toward her on the bed, she pleaded for him to stop.

"You don't want to hurt me! I'm your wife. Remember?"

He stopped and for a second, Kylie thought he might have snapped out of it. Then, he lifted the lamp from the nightstand and cracked it against her skull, sending her toppling over and off the bed.

Waking an unknown time later, she saw Paul across the bedroom pulling up his pants. When he turned his body slightly, she jerked her eyes shut, pretending to still be knocked out. She prayed desperately for the Lord to rescue her, to help her. In her time of greatest despair and when she desired to die more than she wanted to be alive, she felt God was a million miles away. She felt He didn't care. Her faith was weakened by disbelief, but she still prayed in those darkened days.

An hour later, when Paul had crashed on the couch in the living room with the television on, Kylie rose from the floor of the bedroom. She used the restroom, and on her way out, she caught her reflection in the mirror. Too ashamed to look, she was about to turn away and keep going, but a small voice inside nudged her. *Look at yourself.*

Fighting tears, she looked. Her head jerked her eyes away from the reflection, but that voice nudged her again. *Look.*

She did, and burning tears started to flow. Her heart felt absolutely and totally broken. The voice inside pressed again, this time louder. *You're beautiful. You're precious. Don't let him do this again.* She didn't know if it was God or something else, but that day, she went back into her bedroom and packed a duffel bag and left him forever.

BUMMING rides from Florida to Washington, she made it back to her hometown of Spokane in just over three weeks. With nothing but a duffel bag and a determination for a new life, she called up Betty, a sister and best friend from The Faith House. She happened to have a roommate just move out and welcomed Kylie with open arms and an open heart. Kylie was able to get a job at a fast food place just a couple of blocks away from the apartment complex. Over the course of a year, Kylie worked hard and re-enrolled in college. Every time Betty invited her out to the clubs and bars, Kylie would decline, always finding an excuse, usually homework. Kylie knew God didn't want that for her, and she was trying to stay in God's will the best she could. She didn't read her Bible much, but she prayed at night and went to church on Sundays.

One day, after a hard day at work with her jerky boss, Nathan, she didn't tell Betty 'no' when she invited Kylie to the bar. Relaxing and unwinding was attractive to her this time.

At the club that night, she pounded the first drink Betty put in front of her.

"You know, that had like three shots in it and you don't drink." Betty laughed and smiled.

"I'm fine."

"I'm glad to see you finally let your hair down and live a little. Between school and work, all I see you doing is sleeping and eating."

A cheer came from the dance floor. Kylie turned her head toward the crowd. It appeared the crowd over there was having much more fun than Kylie, so she slid herself off the stool. As she walked toward the crowd on the dance floor, she shoved a balled fist into the air. "Let's dance!"

Out on the dance floor, the drink started to do its work on Kylie. A guy beneath the beaming colored lights leaned into her ear. "Let me buy you a drink."

Dancing on her way over to the bar with the man, she twirled her head full of hair back and forth. She felt good, relaxed. Maybe this whole club scene wasn't a bad thing. The man bought her a drink. She downed it quickly. Then he bought three more, and she pounded them. They danced on their way back to the dance floor.

Kylie didn't worry about anything that night. She didn't

know it going into that night, but what followed that evening at the club and after would change her life forever in the form of a little boy whose name would be Peter.

CHAPTER 17

$\mathcal{A}$FTER GETTING ROSE BREAKFAST, KYLIE went searching for dirty clothing throughout Jonathan's house to do a load of laundry. She went through Rose's room, the downstairs bathroom where she bathed, the bathroom upstairs, and then finally Jonathan's bedroom. As she picked up his dirty clothes near the door, she spotted a towel on the dresser. Walking over, she plucked it away and turned, but as she did, a drawing fell to the floor.

Glancing over her shoulder toward the doorway, she made sure he hadn't left his studio and wasn't standing there watching her. Leaning over, she picked it up and looked at the drawing. She noticed the upper part of her tattoo. She touched her neck. Uncomfortable but curious, she set the laundry basket on the bed and studied it as questions began to fill her mind like a bucket of water beneath a leaky roof. *Why'd he sketch it?*

"Hey."

Her insides leapt and the sketch went flying up into the air as she was startled by Jonathan's voice. Whipping around, she saw him standing in the doorway with a pair of gym shorts on and a pair of running shoes. No shirt. His body glistened with manly sweat, and she quickly shifted her gaze to the floor as she proceeded with the basket of dirty clothing toward the door. "I'm so, sorry, Jonathan. Mr. Dunken. I was just in here getting your dirty clothing and noticed the sketch right there." She hastened her steps toward the doorway, hoping he'd step out of the way, but he didn't. He stood blocking the way. As she stood there with her eyes down, the smell of healthy male sweat mingled with his cologne in the air in front of her.

"Notice anything about it?" His inquiry felt like a test.

"Not really." Kylie dipped her head further, trying to motion for him to get out of the way. He obliged, shifting his body to let her by. She was almost to the end of the hallway when he called her name.

"Kylie. What's the tattoo about?"

Her chin shifted over her shoulder. "You have your secrets. I have mine."

Hurrying downstairs, her heart pounded. In the laundry room just off the hallway near Rose's room, Kylie tried to focus her thoughts anywhere but on Jonathan. Why'd he sketch her tattoo? Why'd he have to stand there in his doorway in such a seductive kind of way? She was frustrated. Filling the washer with water and detergent, she started to load the clothing from the basket.

Suddenly, Jonathan appeared in the doorway. Still no shirt. He raised his arm up and leaned against the doorway, his arm muscles bulging as he did so.

"My wife died of cancer."

Pain flicked Kylie's heart upon hearing the words. Stopping mid-motion of moving clothing to the washer, she rested her hands on the rim of the washer and turned her head toward him. She could see the deep pain in his soul by the way his eyes looked at her. She suspected that telling her that took a lot from him. She spoke softly as she replied. "I'm sorry."

He raised a hand. "Please do not try to say something about God and how He works everything together for good. I seriously can't hear another ridiculous line like that again."

"I didn't plan on it." Kylie shook her head, her chin lifting as she peered into Jonathan's eyes. "Do you want to talk about it?"

"Not really."

"Okay. Well, I can relate to you on losing people you care about. I've lost people too, Jonathan. In fact, I'm losing someone right now."

His eyebrows lifted.

"My grandma whom I live with is dying. We call her Grandma, but she's really been my mom my whole life since I was seven." Releasing the laundry in her hands, she came closer. "Jonathan, I understand how it feels like God is ripping someone away from you."

He nodded. "Who'd you lose?"

"Betty. A lady who was practically a sister to me." Kylie pointed to her back. "The night I got this tattoo, I was trashy drunk and I had already made a slew of mistakes before that point. Mind you, I wasn't a drinker even then. I let this guy, who happens to also be Peter's biological father from a mistake that night, take me to a tattoo parlor, and Betty came with us. I was getting tattooed inside, and she was arguing with Peter's dad outside the parlor. He shoved her into oncoming traffic and she died."

Jonathan stood there, not saying a word but shaking his head as tears welled in his eyes. She felt like she'd shared too much too quickly. Then, he surprised her. He took a step closer and put his hand on Kylie's back and then reached in and hugged her. Kylie loved the way his hug felt. It warmed her, and not because his body was heated from his workout.

For a whole second, as they released, she half-expected a kiss, though she wasn't sure why. Realizing her desires were flaring more than ever for him, worry soared within her. Her heart pounded. She needed to escape the situation. "I'd better get this finished and get Rose in the stroller. We're going to the park."

"Oh, neat." He took a step back, nodding as he did. "It should be a nice day for a stroll in the park. Maybe this evening, we can eat out in the backyard at the picnic table?"

"I'd like that. You can grill the chicken I have marinating in the fridge."

"It's a plan."

As Jonathan left her to finish the laundry, she couldn't stay strong. She broke down. Crying silently, she begged God to remove her feelings for her boss. She didn't want to fall for another guy who was image-obsessed. *This job was supposed to be a way out from the job at Ethan's. I thought it was a blessing, but it's quickly becoming a bit more than I wanted. Lord, I need Your help.* After her emotions settled down, she remembered the guy Savannah had emailed her about. She'd be meeting him in a few days. Latching her hope onto that meeting, she started to feel better.

CHAPTER 18

*C*UTTING OPEN THE CHICKEN WITH a knife as it sizzled on the barbecue, Jonathan checked to see if the meat had cooked all the way through. He determined there were about five more minutes to go and shut the lid. Stepping away from the heat of the grill, he walked across the patio and over to where the cement met the grass of his backyard. Peering out into the yard, he watched as Rose, Peter, and Kylie played a game of tag. They all had smiles on their faces, and it caused Jonathan's heart to stir with warmth. He smiled.

The early evening was warm, the sun still high in the cloudless sky. The pleasant weather only added to the joys of the smell of the chicken grilling and the sound of Kylie playing with the kids. Jonathan's mind began to wander. He let himself imagine for a moment that she wasn't just the hired help but something more. His heart felt a certain type of joy it hadn't experienced in years, not since Marie was alive. Kylie turned and looked at him right then, and her smile made his heart begin to pound. He wanted more of her.

"Is it about time?" He heard her words but was lost in the

possible meaning. He shrugged. Leaving the kids in the grass, she walked up to him, perplexed. "You don't know if the chicken is almost done?"

"Yes. Sorry. I spaced." Glancing at the barbecue, he nodded, then looked back at her. "It's a few minutes more." His heart pounded all the more as she moved closer to him. She was only a few feet from him now. He could smell her fruity perfume. When he didn't break eye contact, she did instead and turned to the kids behind her. "I'm glad they get along well together. We'll have to do more things like this. I think Rose really enjoys the company of another child, and I'm sure Peter likes having a pretty girl around him too."

"He already has one of those." Jonathan let his emotions slip a comment in the moment. He tensed up. A blush immediately entered Kylie's cheeks. "Sorry, I didn't mean to make you uncomfortable."

"It's okay, really." Her gaze met his for a moment, then skidded past his shoulder toward the door that led inside. "I'll go get plates and drinks ready for us all."

As she lowered her head and walked past him, his heart longed to pull her into his hold, to kiss her. As the door shut behind him, the nonsense stirring about in his thoughts settled down. Reality set in quickly thereafter as he thought of Marie. He felt bad.

Jonathan soon pulled the chicken off the grill and placed it onto a plate Kylie had set out for him. She had also brought plates and cups, along with a pitcher of ice water to the picnic table in the grass. Sitting down, they both prepared their children's plates first and then their own. Jonathan bit into his chicken straightaway, but Kylie asked if they could pray first. He usually ate dinners alone up in the studio, but each time he did end up joining them at the dinner table, Kylie requested prayer every time.

Everyone bowed their heads, and Kylie prayed. "Thank

You, Lord, for this food. Please bless it to our bodies and bless the hands that made it. Thank You for this beautiful day, and thank You for *friendship* and love and family. Amen."

Jonathan could sense that comment might've been directed at him for his flirty comment that had slipped out earlier. "My earlier comment was totally out of line as your boss. I don't know what I was thinking. I guess I kind of wasn't. You know? I hope things aren't going to be weird between us now. I just realized the fact that I'm apologizing again might just make things that much more awkward."

When she laughed, it helped Jonathan relax and he laughed too. Kylie shook her head. "It's okay, Jonathan. Seriously. I only said friends because I consider you a friend, not just a boss."

He smiled. "I consider you a friend also."

AFTER LAYING Peter down that night, Kylie stretched herself out on the couch at Grandma Faith's with a pint of *Ben & Jerry's* ice cream. Spending the day with her boss and then extending it into the evening for dinner had exhausted her. She was quickly coming to terms with the reality that Jonathan certainly had an interest in her, and she already knew she did in him, but she couldn't help but question her judgment in men. She had wasted such a great deal of time, and life, in her marriage to Paul. She had also made a mistake with Peter's father that night at the club. She couldn't convince herself of Jonathan being a part of God's will in her and Peter's lives.

The door to Grandma Faith's bedroom closed, and soon Jenny walked out into the living room. Dropping into the recliner beside the couch Kylie was on, she let out a heavy sigh.

"She's getting so weak, Kylie. I'm fearful the end is near."

Kylie sat up and set her pint of ice cream down on the coffee table. "I hope I have the strength of faith she has when my time comes."

"Right? I really admire her for it. Hey, so tell me, how did your night go with the boss-man? You seemed pretty excited when you swung by earlier to pick up Peter."

"It went well. He flirted with me. I think it was by accident, but it still happened."

"I knew it!" She sat upright in the recliner. Coming to the edge, she leaned toward Kylie. "Tell me. Do you like him?"

Her heart pounded. Of course she did, but she didn't want to admit she had fallen for her boss. "Yes, but I fear he doesn't take God seriously. And he's my boss, Jenny. I couldn't pursue anything with him."

"Be his friend."

"I am being his friend."

"Then just see where it takes you."

"I will. I think I'm going to make some tea. Want some?"

"Sure."

Leaving the living room, Kylie entered the kitchen. She pulled down the tea bags from the cupboard and a couple of cups. Running the water, she filled the cups and set them in the microwave. Crossing her arms and leaning against the counter as she waited for the water to warm, she thought of Jonathan and the time together earlier, both the time in the laundry room and in the back yard. She thought about the delicate way he had spoken to her about death. Her emotions stirred within her the more she thought of his words. The microwave dinged, letting her know the water had heated.

Steeping the tea on the counter, she continued to let her mind dwell on Jonathan. An image entered her mind as she tapped the hot spoon against the inside of a cup as she stirred in sugar. He was at his drawing desk in his studio when suddenly, she walks in. He drops his pencil and rushes across the floor to her. They embrace in a deep kiss. Then suddenly, the image broke from her mind as hot water spilled over the edge of the cup and splashed onto her skin.

This desire for Jonathan was growing, and she didn't know if she could stop it. They spent every day together. She ended the mental image of him and her and bowed her head to pray. *Lead me, Lord. Please.*

CHAPTER 19

*J*ONATHAN HEADED TO TYLER'S PLACE over off Grover Street in Spokane on Saturday. His brother had an oversized studio apartment that sat above the bowling alley he owned. It was modest, but he refused to give it up, and he liked to keep an eye on the employees. Jonathan carried Rose up the narrow, poorly-lit stairwell to the apartment. He adjusted the backpack on his shoulders as the sound of pins being bowled over could be heard below. Arriving at the top of the stairs, he knocked on the door.

The door opened. "Brother, come in." Tyler held open the door as he and Rose crossed the threshold into his house. As Jonathan set Rose down, Tyler raised an eyebrow. "There are lots of breakables. Maybe keep her in the living room only?"

Rose was already dashing over to the nearby bookcase and reaching for his signed *Babe Ruth* baseball.

"How do you suppose I do that?" Jonathan asked with a sarcastic laugh as he hurried behind Rose. He scooped her up into his arms and set the cased baseball back down on the shelf. He carried her into the living room. "I did come prepared though."

Loosening the backpack off his shoulders, he swung it around to his front and set it on the carpet in the living room. He pulled out her dolls and a couple of the Christian books that Kylie had given her. Bending a knee, Jonathan grabbed her hand gently. "Leave Uncle Tyler's stuff alone and play with your stuff only. Okay, Rose?"

She nodded and immediately went for a book.

With his arms crossed and a smile curling his lips, Tyler watched Jonathan as he stood up and came over to him. "You're really digging this Dad thing, aren't you?"

Jonathan and Tyler went over to the dining room table. Opening his arms, Jonathan smiled as he sat down. "I think I am."

Hesitation lingered on Tyler's lips and Jonathan noticed it.

"Go ahead."

Leaning slightly across the table as he clasped his hands together, Tyler lowered his voice. "Marie would've been happy to see you like this, brother."

"Being a dad?" Jonathan shrugged. "I agree. I just wish she was here to do this with me."

"Yes, the help would be nice, but really, she'd be happy seeing you enjoying life again."

Jonathan tilted his head, looking at his brother as he felt a bit puzzled. "I'm lost."

"Come on, man. You've been depressed for years. You and I both know you sank your life into your work after you lost Marie. Sure, it was a startup, but you really closed up. Now? You're happy, and I think it's all because of that girl."

Jonathan smiled as he looked over at Rose. "Yep. That girl right there has my heart in her little hands. She's changed my life."

"I know Rose has, but I'm talking about Kylie."

He jerked his head toward Tyler, surprised to hear him mention her. "What? Why would you think that?"

"She's hot. You know she is. That's why you picked her up at the restaurant, right? Wait, do you mean you two aren't dating yet?"

"No, we're not dating. And don't talk like that about her."

"Little defensive of the nanny, aren't you?"

Jonathan raised his hands "Look, I'm just saying don't call her *hot*. Calling women that is immature. Sure, Kylie is an attractive woman, but I'm keeping it professional between us." He wasn't ready to tell anyone about how he felt about Kylie, not even his brother. He couldn't do that to the memory of his wife. It'd dishonor her.

"Okay." Tyler went silent, studying Jonathan for a moment before he spoke again. Finally, he shrugged. "In that case, I'm going to ask her out."

"No, you're not."

"Why? You don't have any interest in her, so what's the issue?"

Jonathan's shoulders sagged. Hiding the truth wasn't going to be easy with his brother, the only person in the world who really knew him. "Okay! I like her. It's just hard to admit out loud that I have feelings for someone. You know? I lost Marie, and I swore I'd never love or like another woman again. I feel like I'm betraying her in some way by having developed feelings for someone else."

Tyler's expression softened. "It was *until death do you part* with her, brother. That was your vow. I know you loved Marie and probably still do, and what you had with her will never go away. But we both know how Marie felt in those final days about your moving on."

Jonathan's eyes glistened hearing Tyler talk about Marie. He hadn't properly grieved for his wife. The only grieving process he'd really had was behind a closed door with a sketch pad and a pencil in isolation. The notebook titled *Pain* still sat under his mattress in his bedroom and was filled with sketches from that period of time before and after Marie passed.

"Think about what you'd gain." Tyler pulled his chair closer to the table, leaning toward Jonathan. "Think about having a wife again, Jonathan. Not right this second, but eventually. Being loved and loving."

A tear fell from Jonathan's left eye and he wiped it. "I have thought of it. I want that again, Tyler. I do. I just don't know how to get it and be okay with it within myself at the same time."

The tattoo flashed through Jonathan's mind right then, and he thought of Kylie's past. "Plus, why risk everything? There's a lot more to Kylie than I even know. Sure, she can change a diaper and love on a child, but can she really commit to a life with someone? I'm not looking for a fun little dating relationship. I think of the bigger picture."

"You always have."

"Right. And Kylie has a two-year-old son who wasn't from her marriage. I just don't know. I don't have all the information I need."

"That's why you learn more about her. I'm not saying go in on Monday morning and propose to the gal. Get to know her. Relationships require us to invest in another human being. To get to know them."

Jonathan tipped a nod in agreement. He knew getting to know her more was something that needed to happen if he wanted to entertain the idea of a future with the woman. Thinking of his upcoming trip out of town next month for work, this time to *Ocean Shores*, he wondered if she would possibly travel with him. It'd give him a chance to get to know her more.

"You bring that proposal for Elliot?" Tyler shifted the topic to business after a minute of silence.

"Yes, of course." Standing up from the table, Jonathan went over to the backpack and lifted the proposal from the compartment located in the front. As he flipped it open, he saw a note from Kylie that brought a smile to his face and a warmth to his heart.

Hope you're having a good time with your brother.

Kylie

SATURDAY EVENING, Kylie did her best to listen to Cory, the man whom Savannah had invited to the singles gathering, go on and on about the latest historical novel he had read from the eighteenth century. Kylie was fighting sleep as she tried to pay attention to him at the small table they were sharing. When he paused to take a drink of water, she perked up at the opportunity to speak and possibly steer the conversation away from reading.

"Kind of cool how God brought all these believers under one roof. Right?"

Nodding in short bursts, he surveyed the room and then adjusted his tie. "God is always working and moving in ways we cannot even fathom. It's so fascinating that I can see God's influence in a situation in one moment, only to turn around and see Him in another. It's like He is super-aware."

Kylie felt herself drawn to this conversation much more

than his novel reading. She took a drink of her soda and then set it back down on the table. "It's hard to imagine how God is everywhere at every moment and aware of everything. Thinking about time and space being finite and having a beginning is incomprehensible."

"Exactly. Our brains and bodies were born into this limited dimension so we cannot even begin to fathom anything outside it."

Kylie smiled genuinely for the first time that night. She enjoyed speaking with Cory about things related to God. She felt they were on the same wavelength when it came to the topic of God. When the organizers finally announced they were about to close up and send everyone home, Kylie then realized they had spoken for three hours. The first twenty minutes took forever, but the rest of the evening's conversations about faith, love, marriage, and other related topics to God kept her engaged and unaware of time while she spoke with Cory.

"We should get together again." Cory's comment came as they stood up and helped stack chairs on the far side of the fellowship hall at the church. Kylie nodded in agreement as she carried her chair over to the stack. Cory took her chair from her hands and stacked it for her. Turning back to Kylie, he smiled. "How about Thursday at seven? We can go grab a bite and a movie?"

"Sure." Kylie smiled. Gently grabbing his hand, she gave it a squeeze. "It was nice talking with you tonight, Cory."

Savannah tortured her with questions on their way out to the parking lot to their cars. She wanted to know all the details until she found out they'd spoken of nothing other than God. Kylie beamed. "He was really nice."

"*Nice*. You keep using that word when talking about the guy." Stopping between their cars beneath the street light,

Savannah grabbed her hand and looked at her straight on. "Why do you keep referring to him as *nice?*"

Kylie shrugged. "I don't know. I'm going to go out with him this Thursday. Have to see where things go."

Savannah agreed and got into her car. After Savannah pulled out of her parking stall and left, Kylie was left alone with her thoughts in her car. She rested her forehead against the steering wheel as reality set in. She had loved Cory's personality and desire for all things God, but there wasn't any chemistry between them physically, at least not for her. She started to tear-up as she squeezed the steering wheel in her car. *How can not having a physical attraction to him matter, Lord? He's a good man and someone who would be perfect for Peter to have as a role model. What is wrong with me?* Wiping her eyes after praying, she turned the key over and resolved that she'd keep trying with Cory. Maybe God could help out and put an attraction there that Kylie wasn't feeling toward Cory at the moment.

CHAPTER 20

ONE EVENING AFTER DINNER THE following week, Jonathan asked Kylie if she wanted to pick up Peter and they could all walk down to the park a few blocks away in the neighborhood. She agreed and so the four of them headed down the sidewalk. He needed to get out of the house and clear his mind for a bit. He suspected a journey to the park with the kids could do just that.

"It's so nice out this evening. I love the warmer times in the year." Kylie's eyes were closed, her chin held up as she let her skin soak up the rays of sunshine.

"I agree. Everyone is out of their houses and away from all the digital junk in the world. Riding their bikes, going to playgrounds, and playing sports." Recalling his work life being the dominant force for so long, Jonathan's shoulders sagged. "Honestly, before the two of you came around, I didn't spend much time in the sunshine, even when it was warm."

Kylie lowered her chin and opened her eyes as she peered his way. "Well, you have us now, and you're walking to the park."

"That's very true."

As the four of them entered the entrance to the park, Kylie grabbed hold of both children's hands and they sprinted toward the playground. Jonathan laughed seeing Peter and Rose giggling excitedly as they ran with her.

The children were happy. He was happy.

Taking a seat on a picnic table beneath a shelter a few feet from the playground equipment, Jonathan took in the scene as the children, along with Kylie, climbed through tubes, crossed over bridges, and rang a bell before going down the slide. He appreciated the fact that the playground didn't cost a dime, and it brought such joy to each one of their lives. He also loved seeing the other kids showing up intermittently through the hour and a half they were there.

Kylie, too worn out, walked through the park off the jungle gym and over to the water fountain attached to the building that housed the restrooms. After getting a drink, she joined Jonathan at the picnic table, plopping down right beside him.

"Rose has a kind heart. Did you know that?" Kylie looked over at him, waiting for an answer as she caught her breath.

He immediately thought of not Shawna, but Marie. "It runs in the family."

Kylie pointed out Peter. "That boy is going to be an athlete. He sprints non-stop and has a competitive spirit like none other."

Jonathan snickered. "Boys, scratch that, *all men* tend to be competitive by nature. I remember this one kid in third grade. His name was Robby Calten. Anyway, Robby and I would race to the doors after recess every day."

"Every day, huh? Who won?"

Jonathan's expression turned smug as a grin sneaked in the corner of his mouth. "Who do you think?"

Kylie laughed, falling slightly against him, her hand brushing his arm.

~

JONATHAN STOOD up from the picnic table and helped Peter into a swing designed for smaller kids. Once he was buckled into the seat, he pulled the swing back and gave him a good push, sending him whooshing through the air. As Kylie saw this all unfold, her heart warmed with a warmth she hadn't felt before. There was something beautiful about a man who took the time to play with children.

Feeling her affections grow, she prayed. *Dear, God. He's my boss. Please don't let me feel this way about Jonathan. Please help me in this time of need. I need You more than ever.*

As they left the park and started down the sidewalk a little while later, the sun was starting to go down across the tops of the neighborhood trees. A beautiful mixture of oranges, reds, and even a few out-of-place blues filled the sky, topping off what was considered by Kylie to be the perfect way to spend an evening.

"This was fun." Her smile radiated the warmth she felt in her cheeks as she glanced over at Jonathan.

He raked a hand through his hair as he nodded. "It was a great way to spend some free time. The kids weren't even naughty the whole time!"

"Every perfect gift comes from above."

He smiled and tossed a thumb her way. "Bible-verse lady over here."

She laughed. "I prefer 'Jesus Freak.' Honestly, though, I do believe the Scriptures, and it says every good and perfect gift is a gift from God. How can you look at that sky, Jonathan, and not feel it is a gift from God Himself? You know God did it."

"I'll concede that. The art that naturally occurs is quite breathtaking."

"All right. Good." Smiling, Kylie felt a sense of victory over the matter.

CHAPTER 21

*I*T TOOK THREE WEEKS FOR Jonathan to work up the courage to ask Kylie to join him on the business trip to Ocean Shores. He had plans of leaving tomorrow, and his time to ask her was running thin. It would be barely enough time for her to make plans for Peter, in the event she were to accept. Part of him felt she'd decline, but he couldn't get asking her out of his mind. He knew he'd regret it if he didn't at least try. So before she had arrived for her day of work that Thursday morning, he stopped early on the treadmill and took a shower in preparation for speaking with her.

His hair still wet, he went downstairs wearing a pair of dark jeans and a button-up blue and black flannel shirt. Entering the kitchen as she was putting on a pot of coffee, she jumped a little when he accidentally bumped over a coffee cup sitting on the counter as he walked toward her. He grabbed at it as it tumbled, luckily catching the cup mid-air. He placed it back in its position on the counter and turned to her.

"Hey, I wanted to ask you something."

"Okay . . ." Her eyes darted back and forth. She appeared nervous.

"You know how I'm going to Ocean Shores this weekend for business?" He hoped the mention of it being a business trip might settle her resistance that he sensed she would have in the conversation. "I was wondering if you could possibly come with me? It'd be nice to have an extra set of eyes on the beach."

"I'm not an architect, so no, I'm sorry." She walked past him and to the sink to fill the coffee pot with water. He studied her, trying to read her body language, but she wasn't giving anything away easily.

He tried again. "You have an eye for detail. I think it'd be helpful. Plus, you could watch Rose so I don't have to leave her."

She shut off the water, paused, and then turned to him. She peered into his eyes, as if she was trying to read him now. "I have Peter to think about, not just myself here. I was promised weekends off, Jonathan, and I've been more than generous with my time as it is, staying late when you have to go meet a client or to see your brother."

"Tyler, my brother and *partner*. But yes, I know what you mean. I just thought . . ."

She stopped him with a raised hand. "If I can decline, I'd prefer that. Plus, Cory and I are going over to Coeur d'Alene this weekend to go boating."

Jonathan's wind was knocked out from his lungs by the mention of another man. He didn't want to force her to go on the trip. He merely wanted to test the waters. "Cory? I haven't heard of him."

"He's a guy I met a few weeks ago at a singles' thing at church. He's a great guy. Really great man of God."

Did she have a boyfriend this whole time? Jonathan's heart took a huge jump backward and his defenses shot up. It was apparent to him now that this attraction and desire were one-sided. "I'd love to meet the lucky guy sometime. You should bring him by."

"Really?" She seemed apprehensive for a moment, then it shifted to excited. "That's a great idea!"

Becoming uncomfortable, he excused himself to his studio to work. Opening his drawer in his desk, he looked at the tattoo sketch he had made and then took it to his bedroom. Lifting the mattress, he retrieved his notebook and slipped it inside. It was time to distance himself from her. If she was seeing someone else, he felt this attraction he had toward her had to be only one-sided.

KYLIE WAS FLUSTERED over her choice of words with Jonathan earlier that day. She had been dumb and tried to flaunt her not-even-a-boyfriend in front of him. *Why'd I do that? Am I trying to push him away?* Then she reminded herself of his lack of interest in God. *Yes, you are trying to push Jonathan away.* She had been with Cory on several dates now, and things were going okay, yet when she was honest, she knew there was still no attraction. In fact, she actually had plans to break up after their trip to Coeur d'Alene to go boating. She didn't want to lead the poor man on knowing she hadn't the faintest attraction to him physically. Jonathan, on the other hand, was nothing but attraction and tension and heat. It was an unseen force between them she had to constantly ignore and push out of her mind. Part of her worried whether breaking things off with Cory would make her do something wrong with Jonathan.

That evening, when she was about ready to leave for home, she walked into the kitchen to grab her purse when she saw his suitcase sitting in the doorway leading toward the foyer. Jonathan walked in a moment later.

"I thought you were leaving tomorrow morning."

"I was, but I decided to do some night driving and get a head start. I'm going to drop Rose off at Tyler's and head out of town. I offered him my house to watch her, but he insisted on his place. I think he really enjoys being an uncle."

"That's great about Tyler. Why do you like night driving?"

"I don't. I want to see the sunrise while my toes are buried in the sand." He smiled. "It's something I haven't done in a while, and I want to do it again."

Her heart melted thinking about him being alone on that beach come sunrise. Her heart pulled toward wanting to go just like it did earlier when he asked, but she kept fighting against the current. Then, she let go and let her thoughts drift downstream. She imagined the sunrise coming up and her and Jonathan holding hands. She pictured how it could feel to be standing there with him. Her lips curled into a smile at the thought. "Sounds amazing."

He crossed the kitchen to her and gently grabbed hold of her arms. "Then come with me, Kylie."

She started paddling up stream, against the current. "I can't."

"Why? Are you worried I might try something? I'm not that kind of guy. I don't go for taken women."

"No." In her heart, Kylie held a hope he would try something like a kiss if she were to go, but her heart also didn't want any more emotions to stir for this man. She knew the heart could be deceitful and this could all be bad. After all, she was horrible at picking the right guys. Her heart started to pound, almost about to give in. Then a thought surfaced, a pure and honest thought. *God is important to you, Kylie. God isn't important to him.* The fight within her settled and she was able to relax herself. She desired not only a man in her and her son's life but a man who cared about God. Not only because she did or because he was raised in a church all his life, but because that man's heart had truly surrendered to Jesus. Maybe it was unrealistic for her to desire such a man, but even so, she wasn't about to choose to be put in a tempting position by traveling with Jonathan.

She forced a sad smile. "Have a safe trip, Jonathan."

Jonathan tipped her a nod, grabbing his suitcase off the counter. "Thanks. Lock up when you leave." Leaving the kitchen, he went into the living room and scooped up Rose and the backpack with her stuff in it and left. As the door shut, she walked over to the kitchen table and sat down. Then, she prayed.

CHAPTER 22

JONATHAN - AGE 17

*I*T WAS SENIOR YEAR AND the final days of school were upon the senior class of Mount Vernon High. Jonathan and his sweetheart, Marie, were looking toward the future with an eagerness and determination to not only marry next month but be happily married for decades to come. Jonathan had already been accepted into his top pick of colleges, *Whitworth University* over in Spokane, Washington, roughly three hours from Missoula, Montana. Marie had a job lined up with her aunt Veronica at her flower shop in downtown Spokane. He'd go to school during the day while she worked and they'd come together at home in their apartment right off campus. They had a plan for their life.

"Settle down, class. I know you're excited, but you still have a week left." Mr. White made his attempt to settle his Creative Writing class full of seniors. Standing in front of the class, he wrote a poem on the board. Then he offered the first person to guess who wrote it a candy bar of their choosing.

Many of the kids were still chatting with one another and

barely heard what the teacher was saying up front, but Marie, who sat by her own choice in the front of the class, raised a hand. Jonathan loved her quiet demeanor and love for learning. Mr. White called on her. "Marie."

"Whitman."

"Very good. Come claim your prize."

Jonathan studied her as she slipped out from her seat and walked up to the table in the front of the class. Her fingers glided over each candy bar, inspecting them individually. She'd pause, pick one up and read the back of it, and then set it back down, moving on to the next. They were simply candy bars, but to Marie, it was a decision, and she took no decision in life lightly. Jonathan loved her mind and how it was never quick to make a judgment on any one thing. It was so contrary to him. He'd make snap judgments just to hurry things along. Marie was the one of the two who kept their relationship pure, insisting on waiting for marriage and never relinquishing power over to hormones.

WALKING HOME FROM SCHOOL, Jonathan held Marie's hand. They walked below the willow trees as they journeyed down the sidewalk. With Marie's eyes on them, she couldn't wipe the smile off her face. "I love willow trees."

"They're pretty neat."

Nodding, she glanced over at Jonathan, meeting his gaze for a moment. "You going to church tonight?"

Jonathan shrugged, adjusting his books under his arm. He didn't care for church a whole lot, but he knew it meant a lot to Marie so he went regularly. He knew God existed, believed Jesus even died on the cross, but he didn't take his walk as seriously as Marie did and they both knew it.

"You should come. There is going to be a new series of sermons on the fruits of the Spirit. Do you know the fruits?"

"Love. Um . . ."

"Peace, patience, joy, kindness, goodness, gentleness, faithfulness, and self-control." Jonathan couldn't take his eyes off her soft pink lips. He was far more interested in her than talking about what the sermon was pertaining to tonight. He came closer and kissed her cheek, then her neck. She stumbled, giggling as he tickled her neck.

"You make that sound way more interesting than any pastor could. Let's go to the grove and make out for a while. I don't have to be home until four."

She shoved his shoulder as her eyebrows furrowed. "I can't be alone with you. You know that, Jonathan."

"Okay, okay. Sorry."

"I know you're a seventeen-year-old boy, but could you not act like it for once?"

Jonathan stopped, deeply offended by her comment. "What's that even mean, Marie?"

"Don't call me that!" Jonathan never called her Marie but always sweet affection-filled names such as *my love*, *babe*, or *honey*. He only used her name when he was upset.

"Why? It's your name."

Her eyes glistened with tears. "You're rude, Jonathan Allen Dunken!" She darted off down the sidewalk without him and went home. Jonathan continued walking with a furrowed set of eyebrows and guilt weighing on his heart.

AN HOUR LATER, Jonathan walked down the street to Marie's house right around the corner from his parents' house. Knocking on the door, he took a step back and wiped his sweaty palms on his pants. *Please don't be her dad. Please don't be her dad.*

Mr. Gillshock opened the door.

"Pastor." Jonathan tipped a polite bow of his head. "Is your daughter home?"

He crossed his arms. "What's it to you, boy? Marie came running home this afternoon with tears in her eyes. I reckon you put them there." Just then, Marie's little sister Shawna walked up beside her dad and glanced out at him, glaring.

Jonathan ignored her, directing his attention to the pastor. "That's why I'm here, sir. I want to apologize to her."

Squinting as he studied Jonathan, as if he was trying to determine if he should allow his daughter to come out to talk to him, he finally huffed. "Fine. Just a minute." The door latched shut and Jonathan wiped his hands on his pants again. Pastor Gillshock had a way of belittling anyone who had thoughts opposite to him and made a habit of making sure Jonathan felt like he wasn't good enough for his daughter. He didn't forbid them to marry, but he had advised Marie against it.

A few moments passed, and then the door opened once more. Marie slid out from the small opening and shut the door behind her. They walked over to the porch swing and sat down. Kicking off from the porch, the two of them sat in silence as the swing swung slightly. Jonathan broke the silence after a minute.

"I'm sorry for earlier. I didn't mean to upset you. I just love you so much and I love to kiss, and it's really hard to wait for next month. You know what I mean? I feel myself thinking it's only next month and then we're married. What's the big deal? Right? But my mind is working against me constantly."

Wiping a tear, she nodded. "I know you think that way.

Just respect my wishes. I want the blessings from waiting, Jonathan. Do you understand that?"

"Yeah, we'll die if we do anything before marriage."

She shook her head. "No, we wouldn't *die*. We'd have to reap what we sow though." Resting her hand on his hand, she caught his gaze. "We're going to have the rest of our lives together. It's better this way, and I know you know it's true. Hey, I got you something the other day at the flea market. Wait here."

Leaving the porch swing, she went inside for a minute and then came back out with a double-stranded gold necklace. He smoothed his thumb across the reflective gold strands. Peering up into her eyes, he felt his heart warm.

"I was going to wait until we were married to give it to you." Coming closer to Jonathan, she sat down and leaned toward him as she pointed to each strand. "Each of the strands represent one of us in marriage. We're getting married and we are becoming one flesh, just like the Scriptures say happens. This is a symbol of that, Jonathan."

"That's awesome, babe. Thank you." Wrapping his arms around her, he hugged her. He would do anything for her, even wait for marriage, if that's what she wanted.

CHAPTER 23

*K*YLIE HAD FORGOTTEN TO FOLD the clean clothes in the dryer, so the next morning, she phoned Jonathan to make sure it was okay if she went back over to his house and let herself in. He was fine with it.

Once inside, she felt an eerie feeling settle over her. His house was quiet, each room full of only silence. There was no Rose, no Jonathan, and no television on. It carried a coldness she hadn't felt before, and she couldn't help but think of how things must've been before Rose had entered his life. *He must've been lonely.*

Hurrying to the laundry room, she pulled out the clothes from the dryer and took them into the living room to fold. After she was finished, she took the pile for Jonathan into his bedroom. As she walked in, she tried to keep her eyes straight ahead. It was his bedroom, after all. A private place. Setting the pile of shirts down on the bed, the pile toppled over, sending one over the edge of the bed and onto the floor. When she reached over to pick it up, she saw the corner of a notebook sticking out from underneath the mattress. *What's this?*

Her heart pounded as an open forum of debate launched in her head. She succumbed to curiosity. There was no way of resisting the urge to know more about the man. After all, what she didn't know was holding her back from pursuing anything with him. Carefully, and with a bad gut feeling, she lifted the mattress and pulled it out. She opened it.

Sketches, lots of them, filled each page. A furnace in a dark room, swirling blackness around it, splashes of red and orange colors bursting from the fire. An uneasy sensation filled her as she turned the page. A woman crying, the tears an aqua blue, shimmering with white reflections, the woman herself only a black and white stencil. Kylie wondered who it was, then turned the page again. A woman lying in a bed with a red and black plaid blanket draped over her. Questions etched in sharp black ink circled the woman on the bed in the sketch. *Why'd this happen? How is this God's will? When will the pain stop? When will the sorrow cease? Why, God?* Kylie's eyes warmed with hot tears and her legs weakened. She sat on the edge of the bed. She couldn't bear anymore and shut the notebook. She knew more than ever that she shouldn't have looked. *That had to be his wife.* She wiped the burning tears from her cheeks and put the notebook back where she had found it.

Leaving his bedroom, she closed the door quietly. Her heart ached in a new way for Jonathan. She knew previously that his wife had passed from cancer, but she didn't know the details. Judging by the sketch, it was slowly. Kylie's affection for Jonathan grew to a new depth. Her heart was breaking for him. She couldn't shake imagining how he had sat by his dying wife's side day after day, knowing the love of his life would soon slip into eternity forever. The pain that must've caused was unfathomable.

Would my faith, too, end under the circumstance? She hoped not.

After putting away all the laundry, she returned the empty basket to the laundry room. As she exited his house, she stopped and held onto the door frame. Then, she prayed for Jonathan. *Lord, I know you understand him a lot more than I do. Can you please help his aching heart? His troubled mind? There's a connection I feel between the loss of his wife and the loss of his faith that only You can see and truly understand. You judge the heart of men, not the surface I see. I don't need him to get fixed for me, Lord. He needs to get fixed for himself. Lord, if it is Your will, let it be done.*

WALKING THE BEACH, Jonathan looked out at the crashing waves as they lapped the shoreline that early morning after the sun had risen. Seagulls flew overhead, squawking at one another like an old married couple who bickered all the time. Everything at the beach was in movement. The waves, the birds, the clouds, and even a lone man out walking his dog in the wet part of the sand.

Jonathan came to a stop and stood still. As he did, loneliness invaded him. He didn't have Rose with him to keep his mind distracted now, and he didn't have his work to do it either. Worst of all, he didn't have Kylie. There was just him and his thoughts now. He didn't reveal it to Kylie, but seeing the ocean always reminded him of God. Every time he visited, he always re-imagined the creation account in the Bible. He'd watch in his mind how God had separated the land from the water. He always felt that when he was on the shoreline, he was standing in an exact place God had crafted delicately with His own fingertips.

After recalling the creation account and right at that

moment, Jonathan desired to pray, but part of him pushed against it, an attack of thoughts entering his mind. *God doesn't want to hear from a guy like me. He's got a lot more going on than a sad, sappy little ingrate who lost his wife.* He started walking again down the shoreline. A small whisper nudged his spirit, drawing him to prayer.

The man who had been walking his dog was far gone down the beach now. He had disappeared in the horizon. Jonathan glanced around to make sure nobody had arrived on the scene. Then, he let out a desperate scream as he focused his thoughts on God and all the resentment he had built up in himself for over five years. Peering up at the sky, his eyes glistened as he let the pain from his soul exit through his lips.

"You took her from me, God! I wasn't ready and You just took her!" The walls in his heart cracked with hairline fractures. "We had a plan, God." He wept as his heart weakened. "Oh, did we ever have a plan. Then, You made it so I can't have kids! Then You killed her! What did I ever do to deserve all this? Huh? People spit at the mention of Your name and don't believe in You and live prosperous and wonderfully blessed lives. Yet we, who love You dearly, are killed without reason or cause! Why?"

The walls in Jonathan's heart shattered and he fell to his knees. Raking his hair back with a hand, his fingers touched the necklace on the back of his neck as he continued to weep. Furious, he grabbed hold of that necklace and ripped it off, breaking the clasp in the process. Cocking his arm back to throw it into the ocean, he stopped and fell face first into the sand, squeezing the double-stranded gold necklace. His cheek against the cold wet sand, he sobbed. He couldn't let go of the necklace. He couldn't let go of Marie.

Minutes passed before he picked himself up from the sand. He felt oddly better after his tantrum. Traveling down the beach, he made it back to his car. Sitting in the car on the beach, he thought yet again about God. Then he prayed again. *God, I don't know how to talk to You the way I used to, without so much anger. But I'd like to start again, if it's possible. We used to be close, You and I.* His eyes glanced at a couple with their child walking down the beach and his eyes instantly welled with more tears as his heart ached. *What is wrong with me? Why am I crying so much, Lord?* He took a deep breath in and let it out, attempting to relax all the muscles in his body. *I can't be the dad I need to be for Rose without You. I know that. Please help me not feel anything for Kylie anymore if it's in Your will. Help me focus on what's important, You. Do a work in me, Lord, because I know I can't do it with my own strength.*

After a tear-filled and long-winded prayer, Jonathan drove down the beach to the location where his client planned to build the house that Jonathan would be designing. Getting out of the car with his sketch pad and pencil, he shut the car door and looked across the rocky cliff-side where the property sat above the sand. He let his mind's eye begin to build shapes and objects and windows and doors. Sketching as each one formed clearly in his mind, he turned and took into account the ocean view. It would be a perfect and breathtaking ocean view across the upper-level balcony and through the numerous windows pointing out to the ocean. His turmoil and pain from earlier ceased to exist as he continued sketching.

CHAPTER 24

*K*YLIE DID NOT ENJOY A moment that Saturday on Lake Coeur d'Alene. She felt terrible for what she did by looking at those sketches of Jonathan's. The one good thing it did wasn't even good in itself. Now she knew him on a deeper and more intimate level, but she had invaded his privacy. She had no clue she would feel so conflicted from the sketches. She had merely hoped to have more insight into the man. Now, though, she carried a sadness within her that didn't belong to her but to Jonathan. When Cory stopped the boat at about two o'clock that afternoon for lunch, he handed Kylie a bottle of water and part of the sub sandwich he had packed in the cooler for the two of them.

"You seem quiet today." He undid the cap on his bottle of water and took a long drink. "Which is a bit different for you. I'm having fun, but you? Not so much."

She set the bottle of water down beside her on the seat and shrugged. She couldn't explain things to Cory. She knew he'd become suspicious and concerned to know she was going through her boss's things. Nobody would truly be able to understand what she did, not even herself. "I'm just a bit off. Sorry."

He touched his chest. "I didn't do anything wrong, did I?"

Raising a hand, she tipped a smile. "Of course not, Cory. I'm just a little distracted at the moment. Hey, are we still going to the rope swing you told me about?" She hoped a change of topic would help redirect him away from investigating into how she was feeling. Cory was a good guy and wouldn't let it go easily if the talking continued on the current path.

He took a bite of his sandwich as he confirmed the rope-swing visit with a nod. Finishing his bite, he wiped his mouth of the extra mayo that had seeped out and onto his cheek. "I planned to head there next, actually." Studying their surroundings, he then glanced at Peter. "This sun is warm, the water is cool, and the scenery is gorgeous. This life has so much goodness in it that God gives us."

Kylie's heart warmed at the mention of her Savior. God's mention dislodged her sadness. She took in a deep breath as her gaze wandered all around, looking at the trees, mountains, birds, and other people zipping by on boats. "You're right. There's nothing like enjoying the beauty that exists in nature and life."

She did better the rest of the day as they went to the rope swing and then drove more around the lake. She was able to put the situation with Jonathan into the back of her thoughts and not let it ruin the time with her son and Cory. After they loaded the boat back onto the trailer that evening, they pulled it up to the gate to leave. Kylie thought about her and Cory's future, more specifically the fact that she didn't want one with him. It was the third time trying and it was time to cut ties. It bothered her to end things with such a wonderful guy, but she knew it was better to end things now and not later.

As Cory pulled the truck and boat up to the sidewalk in front of Grandma Faith's house, Kylie turned to him. "We need to talk."

He smiled and nodded, as if he already knew what it was in regard to. He raised a hand. "Before you start, I want to say thank you. These three dates with you have been a real eye opener."

"Don't be sweet right now. Please?"

He shook his head. "No, you're misunderstanding me. I know we don't have the physical chemistry, but you've taught me a great deal in our time together, Kylie."

"Really? What could you have learned from me?"

"I learned what I'm looking for. I used to think I wouldn't be okay dating someone with a kid, but I'm okay with that now. I also thought a deep relationship with God wasn't important, but I understand now that it really is important."

Kylie's mouth opened as she smiled. "I'm glad it was helpful and not completely useless. And I agree, God has to be a priority."

She thanked him again for the trip to Coeur d'Alene and for being who he was. She wished him well and he pulled away from the curb. As she walked toward her front door, she peered down the direction of Jonathan's driveway for a moment. *Give me patience, Lord, and allow me to lean only on Your guidance and will in my life. I don't want to mess things up like I always have in the past.*

THE HOTEL JONATHAN was staying at in Ocean Shores had a restaurant attached to it in the lobby. His server set down his glass of ice water and pulled out her note pad and pen. She took down his order of a burger and fries. As she walked away, he remembered meeting Kylie at *Ethan's* for the first time, her surprised and almost fearful look when he offered her the job. Jonathan let out a gentle laugh as he lifted his glass and took a drink of his water. His phone rang.

It was Tyler calling him back twenty minutes after he had tried to call and see how Rose was doing.

"Just got her down. You know I had to remove basically everything off my shelves in the living room, brother?"

He laughed. "I offered you my place, but you insisted she come to yours."

"I know . . . but Rose wanted to pull out the books, the DVDs, the collectible baseball. Everything that wasn't her toys. I'm pretty confident she's part monster. You didn't tell me that."

They both laughed. Glancing at a family sitting in a booth, Jonathan smiled. "She's just a child. Everything is going to be all right. I promise."

He let out a sigh. "I know, I know. How'd it go today at Rim Rock?"

"Good. I have about five solid sketches worked out. They're techy and modern and really stylish. I think he'll like it."

"That's fantastic. Safe travels on your way back."

Hanging up with Tyler, Jonathan paused and laughed again as he thought about Rose giving his brother grief. When the server came back over with his food, he decided to pray over it.

CHAPTER 25

ON MONDAY MORNING, KYLIE LET herself in through the front door. Jonathan's suitcase was in the hallway near the laundry room. Picking it up, she took it with her into the laundry room and emptied the contents into the washer. Seeing some sand on a shirt, she thought of him on the beach alone, walking and his shoulders sagging. Her eyes welled with tears at the sad scene painted in her mind. *What is wrong with me? Why do I care so much?*

"Hey." Jonathan's voice startled her from the doorway of the laundry room. She quickly threw the shirt into the washer and shut the lid. Turning toward him, she perked up and tried to hide the ache she felt for the man. He proceeded into the room and up to her. His hand came up, gently touching the skin of her arm.

She melted at his touch.

"Are you okay? You seem upset, Kylie."

She wanted to tell him the truth, but fear restrained her lips. She shrugged a shoulder and turned slightly. His hand fell away from her. "I'll be all right."

"Everything okay with your grandma?"

Her heart fluttered at the mention of her grandma. She had only mentioned her once to him. "Yes, she's fine for now." *Maybe it's okay if I tell him,* she thought for a moment. "There is something I want to tell you. To talk about."

"Okay, good." He opened his arms. "What is it?"

She hesitated about telling what she saw and instead opened up about her own painful past. "I was married before and my husband abused me badly. I questioned God too about what was happening to me. I was angry."

Jonathan's eyebrows lifted, suspicion resting in his expression. "I'm sorry that happened to you, but why are you telling me this right now?"

Her lips trembled and worry soared to the surface of her heart. "You know how I came over the other morning to finish that laundry?"

He nodded.

"Well, I was putting your shirts on your bed and one fell. I saw the corner of something sticking out from your mattress and I . . ."

He must've realized what it was. He crossed his arms and lowered his head and narrowed his eyes. "You what? Pushed it back under and left it alone. Right?"

Her lips trembled as she sensed his rising anger. Jonathan suddenly turned and left the laundry room. Kylie's heart pounded, and she hurried after him down the hall, pleading for him to stop and talk to her. He did stop, then he turned to her.

"You had no right, Kylie."

"I know, and I'm sorry!" She grabbed hold of his hands as hot tears streamed down her cheeks. "But I did, and I haven't been able to stop thinking about what I saw. I saw a part of you that I haven't seen, and I can't stop thinking about it or stop myself from thinking about you."

He pulled his hands away sharply. "That was personal. It was private."

Their exchange of words was loud enough that it pulled Rose from her sleep and brought her into the hallway behind them. Silence thrust itself between the two of them as they both turned to Rose and softened their expressions. Kylie's heart was still pounding, but she leapt into action to care for Rose. Approaching her, she bent down on a knee and accepted Rose's request for a hug.

Jonathan stood a few feet from her, and she could feel his eyes burning against the back of her head. Rising to her feet with Rose, she looked at Jonathan as she passed him, carrying Rose to the kitchen for breakfast. She poured a bowl of Fruit Loops for Rose, going slowly on purpose in the hope of Jonathan cooling off. After getting Rose breakfast, they left her in the kitchen to continue their conversation in the living room with lower voices.

"I can't believe you did this, Kylie. Don't you think I would've shown you those sketches if I wanted you to see them? After all we've talked about and shared?"

"I understand." Her voice was weak, faint. After a few moments of silence, she lifted her gaze to Jonathan. "So, now what? I'm fired?"

His lips pressed together tightly to form a thin line. Touching his brow as he glanced toward the kitchen where Rose was, he let out a sigh. "No. You're not fired, but you need to respect my privacy. I think you crossed the line and you know it."

"Okay. That's reasonable. I take full responsibility for my bad decision, and I'm sorry." Wiping her stray tears, she straightened up. "I didn't mean to hurt you."

"I know you didn't." He let out a sigh and opened his arms. "I forgive you."

"Thank you." Crossing the distance between them, Kylie

wrapped her arms around him and hugged him. "I won't do anything like that again."

~

JONATHAN COULDN'T FOCUS LONG ENOUGH to work at all on the final design concepts for the Ocean Shores home. His mind and heart kept going to Kylie, going to the fact that she had been abused, then going to the reality that she had seen something that not even his brother had seen. He was upset about it all, very much so, but in a way, it made him feel more connected to her than ever before. In his heart, he knew seeing those sketches wasn't just seeing personal pieces of art work, but essentially, it was seeing a part of his soul. He didn't know what to do, how to handle the situation. The best and scariest thing in the world had happened when she looked at that notebook. Someone had finally seen the real him that existed only inside his mind, and she hadn't run. *What does this mean?*

Late that afternoon, he got a phone call from Tyler letting him know that Nick, the Ocean Shores client, wanted to meet at the property on the beach on the upcoming Thursday so that the three of them could go over the concepts in person.

"How's that going to work with Rose?" Jonathan's anxiety rose up within him.

"Um . . . I don't know. Kylie could keep her, maybe?"

Guilt weighed on Jonathan's heart. He had already left Rose for the weekend and had barely returned home. He didn't want to leave his little girl again so soon. "I'll figure something, and I'll meet you there on Wednesday."

Hanging up with his brother, he pondered the situation as he leaned back in his chair at the desk and rested his hands behind his head. He knew asking Kylie to go with him on the trip would be futile. He mulled it over and over in his head.

Then he sat straight up, an idea surfacing to his mind. *Unless I allow Peter to come.* Did he dare? Two toddlers and a woman in a small, confined space for over seven hours? Sounded about as good as a knife in the eye to Jonathan, but he didn't have many options in the present situation if he wanted her along. She knew him more now. Maybe this time, she'd say yes to traveling. He rubbed the stubble on his chin. After the huge blowout this morning, he worried she might say no again. He tossed the idea back and forth in his mind through the afternoon. Then, at five o'clock, Kylie knocked on the door and came into the studio.

"Dinner is about done."

"Please come in."

She held a look of worry in her eyes and they glistened on her approach. She seemed upset. "If this is about earlier . . ."

He held a hand up. "I need a favor."

Her expression softened. "Oh?" She approached Jonathan as he stood up. "What's up?"

"I need to go back to Ocean Shores to meet this client on Thursday, and I was thinking." He could see worry flash in her eyes before he was able to finish speaking. "I was thinking you, Peter, Rose, and I could all go. I honestly don't want to leave Rose again so soon. You would really be helping me out, and I will triple your pay for this trip."

Worry left her eyes and she tilted her head. "Really? The four of us?"

"Yes. We'd leave tomorrow though. We will take it slow, see some sights along the way so the kiddos aren't overwhelmed, and they might actually have fun. I'm thinking we will take I-84 that runs along the south side of the state so we can see the Columbia River. We stay the night in the Tri-Cities on Tuesday, then get up and drive, stay somewhere

Wednesday, and then be at the meeting and on the beach Thursday night. Then start back home on Friday."

Kylie's eyes widened, joy flickering. He had finally done something right to make her smile. Then suddenly, she took on a concerned, more hesitant demeanor. "We can't share a room."

"Of course not. Just like last time I offered for you to go, separate rooms. I think we'll have you and the kids in one room and me in one by myself."

She laughed, which caused Jonathan to start laughing.

"I'm kidding, of course. Rose will room with me. And I'll pay for it all, of course. It's a business trip and necessary expenses."

"And this is *business*, right?"

"Yes." He wanted to say 'no.' He wanted to tell her the truth, tell her that he couldn't stop thinking about her while he was gone over the weekend, and he wasn't able to even stay mad about her seeing the sketches because who could be mad at her for long? Jonathan also wanted to confess to her how pleased he was that she was coming this time with him, but he didn't tell her any of it. He didn't tell her he loved the way she threw her head back in laughter at his jokes, and he also didn't tell her about how he loved the way she was with Rose. He didn't tell her how he loved the way she smiled and how her nose would crinkle slightly as her face broke into a grin. He couldn't confess how he felt about her while at the same time remembering his time on the beach, how he couldn't let go of that necklace, he couldn't let go of Marie. Kylie didn't deserve someone who was still in love with another woman. She deserved better, someone who could love her with his whole heart. He'd never deny Kylie that love by taking her for himself.

CHAPTER 26

*K*YLIE STOOD BESIDE THE COUCH at her house the next morning as she anxiously awaited Jonathan's arrival in the driveway. Ever since he had invited her and Peter along for the trip yesterday, she'd had second thoughts about it. Sure, he had said it was strictly business, but how likely was it to stay that way? She knew he had some sort of feelings for her, and she knew if he were to make a move, she wouldn't be able to resist him.

Jenny walked into the living room. "You're pacing. Sit down and relax."

"I will be doing plenty of sitting in the car. Plus, I can't sit down. My emotions are all over the place. I don't want to like him, Jenny, but I can't help it."

"Well, spending more time with him on this car trip isn't going to help you not like him."

Kylie's face flushed. She knew Jenny was right. This trip would bring them side-by-side, literally. It was hard enough with Jonathan just randomly showing up in a room over at his house when he took breaks from the studio. Now, she'd be spending time with him, lots of it. They'd be not only sharing time, but meals too. These thoughts only built her anxiousness inside. Leaving the living room, she went to the one place she knew she needed to go—on her knees in prayer.

Getting down on her knees in her bedroom, she clasped her hands together and prayed. *God, I'm scared. He's a distant and cold man, just like my first husband, and he's attractive like him too. I'm not the best at picking men out, and I'm scared of what will happen on this trip.* Peter's hand touched her arm right then, breaking her out of prayer. He lowered himself beside her and folded his hands together like her. Her heart flinched and she felt a longing for a role model for her boy. *Please, Lord. If this isn't Your will, let me know somehow.*

Within minutes of finishing her prayer, the doorbell chimed. She left her room with Peter and went to answer it. As she walked past the recliner, she saw that Grandma Faith had awoken from her nap.

Answering the door, she saw it was Jonathan. Her heart pounded at seeing him. He was wearing a pair of jeans, a white button-up shirt with the sleeves rolled up, and a pair of sunglasses.

"Hi."

"Hello." He pushed his sunglasses on top of his head. "Where are your bags? I'll grab them while you get the car seat in for Peter in the back. I'm not good with those things." He crossed the threshold of the house.

"Down the hall, last room on the right."

Jonathan stopped at the recliner and turned to Grandma Faith. "And you must be the woman who raised such a wonderful woman. Glad to finally meet you."

"Nice to meet you."

Jenny stood up and her gaze met Kylie's. "You didn't tell me he was handsome *and* charming."

A blush crawled up Kylie's neck and reddened her cheeks. "I'll be out at the car, Jonathan."

JONATHAN DROVE the four of them south from Spokane, heading for the Tri-Cities where they'd stop for the night. Jonathan had a fondness for traveling, especially the open road. It gave him the illusion that he had more control over his life than he truly did. The city, he felt, had a way of making him feel trapped in some sort of cage. The tall buildings were the bars, the cement and metal in them only reinforcing the cage that kept the people of the city inside. The further they drove, leaving the city behind them, the more Jonathan felt his whole being relax. His last trip was about speed and work. This trip, at least in his mind, was about connecting with Kylie.

Stopping for a bathroom break for Kylie, Jonathan listened to a portion of his audiobook, *Mere Christianity* by C.S. Lewis. When she climbed back into the car and pulled her traveling blanket onto her lap, he pulled his ear buds out and turned off the audiobook. He put the car into reverse. "Have you ever read anything by C.S. Lewis?"

"Yes. *The Lion, the Witch, and the Wardrobe.* That was him, right?"

"He did write that. Right now, I'm listening to *Mere Christianity.* I'm only able to mentally process and digest small portions of the book every time I listen to it in order to mull it over and savor every bit of it. I was just listening to this portion speaking about the inner man and how we each have one. I already knew that. What I didn't know was that each decision, great or small, that we make affects us and changes us in some way."

"Well, yeah, our actions have consequences. Right?"

"Yes, but I'm not just speaking in regard to the negative side of things. Nor am I speaking of just the *big* stuff. For instance, if you give a panhandler a five-dollar bill, that's no big deal, right? Well, it is, because it changed you by that simple thing. Sure, you might be a nice person and generous, but it still changed your inner man, or woman. Each action and decision we do changes us in some way. Sometimes, that change is small, sometimes big. Do you think God uses these decisions in our lives?"

She was quiet, then she brought her hands to her lap. "Possibly. You're reading a book on Christianity?"

Jonathan took another look at her. "Yes. Why?"

She opened her hands and shrugged. "Well, you called this a business trip. Seems like it has fallen into a personal type of conversation now."

A wry smile crossed his face. "I was just trying to break up some of the silence in the car."

She raised a hand. "It's okay. I do believe God uses the decisions we make in our lives to lead us. It's nice to hear you're doing some seeking of Him. Don't let the quiet nudge go." She didn't say anything for a few miles down the highway. Then she turned to Jonathan. "Can I ask you something?"

"Please do."

"What happened with Marie?"

Jonathan's heart pounded. He shoved the painful memory down. "I can't talk about that right now, Kylie. Plus, the kids are listening, and I don't want them to know such pain in their lives yet."

"Okay." She changed the topic to the kids in the back seat, who were becoming increasingly fussy.

CHAPTER 27

JONATHAN - AGE 29

*P*ULLING DOWN HER FAVORITE RED and black plaid wool blanket from the linen closet in the hallway, Jonathan walked back to their bedroom. His steps were slow on purpose. It hurt to see her in the condition that she was in now. The doctors said she had months, maybe a year if she was lucky. *Lucky. What a bad word for a time like this. There's no luck in it.* A part of Jonathan just wanted her to pass on to glory soon so she could finally be done with the pain. The other part of him never wanted to let her go. And another part wanted to leave with her.

The door creaked on its hinges as he entered. A lone candle flickered on the dresser on the far side of the room. The walls were covered in pictures of their travels, of their exchange of wedding vows, and of the life the two of them had built together. Coming to his metal chair beside the bed, he lay the blanket across her on the bed and grabbed hold of her hand. Smoothing his thumb across the top of her hand, he sat down. Leaning toward her, he smoothed his hand over her hair, brushing the strands away that had fallen over her eyes.

"Hey, love."

She didn't say anything right away, and a twinge of worry crept into Jonathan's heart that she had passed. He jumped up, the chair flinging back against the wall as he did. His heartbeat shot up through the roof.

"I'm fine." Her words were faint, as weak as her body, and he relaxed. She coughed and started sitting up on the bed. He grabbed the chair and sat down as she sat up, her back resting against the headboard.

"I'm glad you're here, Jonathan. I need to tell you something."

Swallowing the lump of worry in his throat, he scooted closer to the bed, peering into Marie's eyes as he took her hands in his. "What is it?"

"As you know, I won't be around much longer."

Jonathan's eyes welled with tears immediately and he begged. "Don't. Don't go there. Don't talk about it."

She coughed and gasped for air. "Listen to me." She took another long breath, then slipped her ring off her finger. "You're young. You still have a lot of life to live."

He bit his lip, trying hard to control his breaking heart inside. He didn't want to hear any of this. He could barely stand how bad it hurt to hear his love talk as if she wasn't on this earth anymore.

"You will find another who will love you, Jonathan, and you will love her. True love would never force you to stay single and miserable after I'm gone." Grabbing Jonathan's hand, she forced it open and then closed it with the ring inside his hand. "You will know when you've found her." His heart broke knowing he'd never have his future with Marie like they had dreamed.

Jonathan and Marie held onto each other that evening and wept. The following night, she fell asleep and never awoke.

~

IT WAS RAINING the day of Marie's funeral. After the services, they had a wake at Jonathan and Marie's house on Practor Street in Spokane. People he knew and some he didn't stood around in his house and spoke in low voices as he stared out the large window overlooking the front yard where they had envisioned their children would play someday.

"Hey, brother." Tyler's voice was somber, his hand warm as it touched the back of Jonathan's blazer. "I just want you to know if there's anything at all I can do for you, I'm here."

The same old lines said when someone dies were even coming from his brother. Jonathan was nauseated by the whole process of death, and that feeling had little to do with the actual death. It was the family and friends he thought he had known as Marie's friends too. These people tiptoed around the subject and avoided talking about her as if she was some sort of annoyance or plague. He wanted to talk about her with all his being. Getting up in front of the church and speaking about Marie for forty-five minutes might've been difficult for him, but it was the best part of the whole service. A part of him felt that when people were speaking about Marie, it somehow kept her alive just a little bit longer.

Marie's father, Pastor Gillshock, stopped Jonathan in the hallway. His eyebrows low, his voice lower, he grabbed his arm. "This is your fault. All of it. Your sins with my daughter killed her, and I'll never forgive you for what you did, boy. You make me sick."

Numb, Jonathan excused himself from his presence and pretended to use the restroom. Once inside, he locked the door and looked into the mirror. Trying to get ahold of his emotions, he breathed in deeply and told himself everything was okay. Then, out of the corner of his eye, he caught sight of an old faded handwritten note in permanent marker from Marie. It was in the corner of the mirror.

*I love you more
than life itself.*

He lost it. Cocking back his fist, he launched it into the mirror, shattering it into pieces. Blood dripped from his knuckles. He grabbed hold of the sink and yanked on it, trying to uproot it from the floor. Unable to budge it, he pulled harder. His hands slipped and he tripped over the side of the tub and smashed his head into the wall. Then, the shower rod and curtain tumbled down, hitting him. Jonathan could hear the faint sound of Tyler outside the bathroom door, but he ignored his voice. His eyes burning with hot tears, he glared at the ceiling and cried out to God as he lay in the tub. "You took her from me! You took her!" Wailing, he covered his face and a deep sadness wrestled its way into his heart, making its home within him.

CHAPTER 28

*T*HEY STOPPED IN KENNEWICK, THE major city of the three cities that made up the Tri-Cities. After getting checked in at their hotel, they went across the street to *McDonald's* to let the kids play on the toys and eat a cheap lunch. As they sat in the play area, Kylie couldn't help but think of how Jonathan was resistant to sharing more about his wife. *Why can't he talk about it with me?* She wondered.

"Wow. Peter is pretty brave going down that slide face first." Jonathan picked up his ice water and took a sip before putting it back down. Every few minutes, the children would appear down the slide or show up in a see-through part of the tubes and wave down to the two of them as they sat in a booth.

"He really is brave. He is all boy." Kylie's eyes lingered on Jonathan as he smiled, watching Peter scurry from the slide over to the tube entrance. She wanted to crack into that mind, shake out all the locked secrets, and then comfort him.

"There's an indoor swimming pool and hot tub at the hotel." Jonathan looked over at her, tapping the table as he smiled. "I'm looking forward to a nice soak. My neck is wrecked."

Laughing, she turned to the playland. "You don't think they'll be tuckered out after this?"

He smiled. "They'll sleep well with a nice swim on top of playing here."

ELECTING FOR A PLAIN PURPLE ONE-PIECE, Kylie had attempted to stay as modest as possible in her selection of a swimsuit when she packed for the trip. After getting her and Peter changed in their hotel room, she joined Jonathan and Rose down at the pool. Entering the double doors into the swimming area, she walked with Peter on her hip around the corner to the pool and hot tub. Jonathan was already soaking in the hot tub, and he lifted his gaze to meet hers as she approached. Rose was sitting on the upper step that led into the hot tub. Her heart pounded seeing Jonathan's hair wet and slicked back, his pecks out of the water, glistening. Sitting more upright as she came to the edge, he smiled.

"The water is perfect, not too cold and not too hot."

Stepping down onto the steps into the hot tub, the water engulfed her calves, the heat of it strong enough to send tingles of slight discomfort radiating into her legs momentarily. She went deeper, the water raised just above her belly button. The water was hot, comfortable after the initial sting. Turning, she set Peter on the steps beside Rose. Then, she sat near the two children but far from Jonathan. Relaxing herself, she breathed out and let the jets massage her back muscles. Her lips curled into a smile. "This is nice."

"When Marie and I would travel, we always made a point to get a hotel with a hot tub. One time, we kept driving another eighty miles just to get a hotel with a working hot tub."

"Sounds like dedication." Kylie's heart warmed at hearing him mention his late wife's name. He hadn't done that before.

He brought his hands up out of the water and smoothed the both of them over his face, wetting his skin. "We were dedicated." She could tell his words held a double meaning. He glided his hands atop the bubbles in the hot tub as he continued. "Her cancer killed her pretty slowly, but also fast in a way. The days felt like years but the weeks passed like seconds. She was gone within six months of her diagnosis. Her dad blamed me for it happening too." A sardonic laugh escaped his lips. "Her dad is a scumbag."

Shaking her head, Kylie could hardly believe what she had just heard. "You didn't kill her, Jonathan."

"I know, but it didn't stop his words from hurting." He went under the water, then came back up a short while later. Wiping his face, his hurt eyes met hers. "I don't think some people understand the pain they inflict on another person when they say something hurtful."

Kylie scooted along the wall of the hot tub, at the same time keeping an eye on the children, and came closer to Jonathan. She knew just how he felt, flashes of her first marriage parading through her mind. "Forgive them, Father, for they know not what they do."

Jonathan nodded. "Jesus is a better man than I." Jonathan peered at Rose. "But maybe He really is doing something in my life and I just can't see it right now. Dan's being a jerk is why Rose isn't with him right now. I don't think Shawna would've left the kid with me if her dad wasn't the way he was, and if that didn't happen . . . I wouldn't have met you."

Her heart stirred, hearing him open up. "You're right."

"And I couldn't imagine life without Rose. I know it's only

been months since she came to live with me, but it feels like forever, and she's my life now."

"God is always working things together for good."

Jonathan agreed with a nod, then lifted himself up out of the hot tub and walked over to Rose and Peter. Scooping them up into his arms, he glanced at Kylie. "Time for the pool?"

She smiled and swam over to the stairs in the hot tub to join them on their way over to the stairs on the opposite side. Jonathan went into the water, each child on an arm. Kylie entered the pool, watching from a distance. Peter became fussy shortly after they entered the pool, but Jonathan assured him he was safe and got him to relax. After a few minutes of playing, he took the kids over to the stairs to play with the other small children. Then, Jonathan began to do laps in the pool.

SWIMMING UNDER THE WATER, Jonathan kept his eyes open just to steal glimpses of Kylie. Her legs were long and pleasant to look upon. Sure, she was hiding the majority of her body with a one-piece, but she couldn't hide those legs. Coming up out of the water a few feet from her, Jonathan pushed his hair back and smiled at her as he made direct eye contact with her. His heart pounded and it took all the self-control he could muster not to do something he would regret, like kiss her.

"I'm glad we decided to swim."

"Me too." She smiled. "I think it turned out okay." Swimming away from him, she went over to the stairs and left the pool. Grabbing a towel from the shelf of pool towels, she joined another mom at a table near the stairs where the children were playing. She fell into light conversation and Jonathan continued to swim laps in the pool.

He came up for air at one end of the pool and glanced at the children, then went back under, pushing off from the wall. As he swam, he closed his eyes. As they were shut, he saw Kylie. He saw her with Rose, saw her with Peter. His attraction, which had only started as lust, was growing into something more.

Reaching the opposite end of the pool, he came up for air again, glanced at Kylie this time, then re-entered under the surface, pushing off again. His eyes closed, he thought of his time on the beach last weekend and his inability to let go of Marie, let go of the necklace. What'd it mean? Could he never let go of the pain and love another woman? He thought of his wife placing her wedding ring in his hand on her deathbed. His heart pounded, and he shot up out of the water, stopping his swim.

He glanced at Kylie, their gazes meeting for a moment, then he turned to Peter and Rose.

Rose held out her hands, wanting him. He swam over to the stairs.

Her little arms wrapped around his neck, settling his uneasy feelings. He felt okay again. Though his heart and thoughts went back and forth about Kylie, they never changed with Rose. He loved her deeply, and he'd never let her or that love go.

CHAPTER 29

JONATHAN - AGE 29

*A*FTER LOSING MARIE AND QUITTING his job at the architect firm, Jonathan lived off the life insurance for a few months. He spent his days watching re-runs of *Gunsmoke* and gorging himself on sweets. He slept and lived on the couch for three months following the loss of Marie. He did everything he could to keep himself from crying, from being reminded of the pain that had seared his soul.

One afternoon, the doorbell rang. He ignored it at first, but then the doorbell kept ringing. Reluctant, he stood up and tied his bathrobe. He raked a hand through his unkempt hair and smoothed a hand over his unshaven face. He hadn't showered in over a week. Stepping over the garbage and takeout boxes, he made his way to the front door.

It was his brother, Tyler. He lifted his shades and set them atop his head.

"Brother, you look like garbage."

Squinting as the sunlight burned his eyes, Jonathan shook his head. "What do you want?"

"I have an idea. Mind if I come in?" Without waiting for

Jonathan to respond, he stepped past him and continued inside.

He shut the door and followed Tyler quickly. "If you'd called beforehand, I could've cleaned up a little."

"I did call, about twenty-five times over the last week. I just gave up and came over." Tyler's eyes surveyed the trash-filled house and turned around to face Jonathan head-on. "Honestly, I figured I was coming over here to find a body, brother. I'm worried about you."

"Get on with the proposal."

"I want us to go into business together. I think we can do well together. With my business-savvy ways and your architect experience and clientele, I think we could have a good thing."

Shooing a dismissive hand through the air, Jonathan shimmied back over to his spot on the couch in his living room. "No, thanks."

"Oh, come on, Jonathan. Take a look around, man! You're losing it."

"I'm fine."

"You've put on at least forty pounds, you smell horrible and your house is a wreck." Tyler's eyes fixed on the TV, then on the coffee table filled with sketches. "Let your mind do something it wants, brother." He came closer, placing a hand on Jonathan's shoulder. "Let your mind design and draw. I know what you're doing here. You're trying to keep yourself from the pain. Let yourself do that by distracting yourself with work."

Jonathan turned to Tyler. His heart softened at the idea of sketching. "Can I just do the designing? No business *stuff*?"

"Absolutely."

Jonathan stuck out a hand and they shook on it.

THREE WEEKS LATER, Jonathan moved to a new house using part of the life insurance money from Marie. The house was more house than he truly needed, but he loved the wide-open spaces and felt the house gave his mind room to think.

After the last piece of furniture was brought into the house, Jonathan and Tyler sat down on the couch in the living room.

Tyler let out a satisfied sigh and smiled over at Jonathan. "I spoke to your old client from the firm."

"Which one?"

"Crese."

Jonathan jolted upright, sitting on the edge of his seat. "And?"

He smiled. "She's ours."

Leaping up, Jonathan fist-pumped and twirled in his living room. "That's great. She'll bring in so much work for us."

Rising to his feet, Tyler opened his arms. "Great news for both of us. See? I told you."

"That you did!"

The next day, when Jonathan was shaving in his bathroom, he noticed his belly hadn't shrunk through the diet change alone that he had taken on the last three weeks. *It's time to bust out the weights and treadmill.*

CHAPTER 30

*W*AKING UP THE NEXT MORNING, Kylie got herself and Peter changed and then headed downstairs to the lobby of the hotel for the Continental breakfast. Jonathan had mentioned the free breakfast on the way up to their rooms last night in the elevator.

Arriving at the dining area, she spotted Jonathan and Rose over near a window on the far side. He had a cup of coffee sitting in front of him and an empty plate on the table. He was sketching. Deciding not to interrupt him, she got herself and Peter a plate of food and approached quietly behind him. Glancing over his shoulder, she studied the drawing. It was of a man and a dog walking down the shoreline of a beach.

Seeing Rose point to them, Jonathan peered over his shoulder. "Good morning." He set the sketch pad down with the pencil and stood up, grabbing chairs from a nearby table. "How'd you sleep?" he asked as he set the chairs in place for us.

"Good. Really comfortable comforters, I thought." Setting

149

Peter down in one of the chairs, she set the plate down and he immediately got to chomping on the grapes.

Kylie went and grabbed a cup of coffee. Returning to the table, Jonathan looked eager to talk as she sat down. "I have a surprise visit planned for today. It's quite spectacular and it highlights a bit of God's handiwork."

"Sounds fun." Buttering her toast, her eyes fixed on the sketch pad. "You sketch a lot in there?" She hoped he'd show her some of his other sketches.

"Yes. Here, take a look." He grabbed the sketch pad off the table and handed it over to her. "Go ahead and look through them all. The ones in there are mostly just fun little doodles and images I have come to my mind randomly. I like to keep a running catalog of what crosses my mind."

Opening the sketch pad, Kylie began to flip the pages. She saw street signs, airplanes, buildings, clouds, and then she paused as she saw one of herself. Her heart pounded. It was a scene of her and Rose out in the back yard from months ago, at the barbecue. That day must've meant a lot for him to sketch it. But why? She looked up at Jonathan.

"Why'd you sketch this one?"

"That was the first day I had felt okay in a long time. I loved having you there, and Peter too. I loved the whole experience of it and I didn't want to forget it, so I sketched it from memory."

A blush entered her cheeks and she closed the sketch pad and handed it back across the table to him. Her whole being was overwhelmed with desire for him. She wanted Jonathan to kiss her, to caress her hair and hold her close to him. She felt her heart slipping further into his gravitational pull. The feeling scared her but continued to pull at her, drawing her in and convincing her that this man was a good man despite the familiar traits of her ex-husband.

"I love how your mind works, Jonathan. The way you see

the world and can put it down on paper is nothing short of amazing."

He smiled, waving a hand through the air. "They're just shadows and shades of reality."

Jonathan's cell phone rang. Glancing at the screen, he mouthed 'Tyler' to Kylie and then answered.

"Yes, we're on schedule." Jonathan smiled at Kylie as he rolled his eyes about the call he was on with his brother. "Yes, Tyler. Uh-huh." Covering the phone, he moved it away from his face and directed his words at Kylie. "He's purely about business. I'm pretty sure he doesn't like the fact that we're making a trip out of it all."

Shortly after getting off the phone, he glanced at his sketch pad. Kylie felt the inclination to continue their conversation.

"That picture you drew of your wife in that bed. It evoked such a strong emotional response within me. I could feel your pain in it."

Jonathan grimaced. "That was a hard piece. I rarely look at it. I like drawing buildings the most, especially designing them. I'm in control, and the building is just that, a building. There are no emotions or pain or sadness."

"Yes, but there's also no life in them."

"That's true, but there isn't any life left in Marie either."

"That's not true. She lives in your memories and she lives on in Eternity."

Rose threw a grape at Jonathan, smacking him in the face and interrupting their conversation. They laughed and began to interact with the children. Kylie wasn't sure what the future held for her and Jonathan, but she resolved to enjoy the rest of the trip and not to worry.

JONATHAN AND KYLIE enjoyed the view out the passenger side window along I-84. The rolling hills, the Columbia River, and the constant reminder of God's creation were everywhere. Finally arriving at their destination that was a surprise to Kylie, they pulled off onto the exit. *Multnomah Falls*, one of the most beautiful waterfalls west of the Mississippi, if not the most breathtaking. They got out of the car and started down a walking path toward the bridge that would cross directly in front of the largest of the falls. The closer they got, the louder the falls became. Jonathan stole glances of Kylie as she took in the nature all around, the trees, the plants, and even the other tourists who were there.

"Isn't this awesome?" Jonathan's gaze fixed on her.

"It is." Kylie's eyes came down from the green lush trees and to him. Her mouth tipped a smile. They all four continued up the path, finally arriving at the bridge. Kylie's mouth gaped open as she approached the cement railing. Jonathan pulled his sketch pad and jotted down a quick sketch of her holding hands with a kid standing at each side of her at the railing. Then he sketched the falls themselves. Putting his sketch pad away in the backpack on his shoulders, he walked up to the railing and stood beside Kylie, just sharing the awe and silence with her. He was comfortable, yet he still wanted more. He almost kissed her right then but stopped himself. His wife's face showed up in his mind and guilt weighed on his heart.

"Are you okay?" Kylie must've sensed his uneasiness. Though he hadn't leaned in to kiss her or anything of that nature, she could read him enough to know something wasn't right. He couldn't dare tell her the truth, to tell her that all he can think about is Marie every time he thinks of doing something more with her.

"I'll be fine. Hey, I saw they were selling cotton candy

down below. You want to head back and we'll get some for the kids?"

"Sure."

On their way down the path from the bridge, Jonathan was thankful that she didn't press more to learn about his sudden uneasiness.

After he bought the kids cotton candy, Kylie turned to him. "So, can I ask you a personal question about your faith?"

"Sure."

"Where you are at with your faith? You went from no mentions of God to lightly mentioning him and listening to a book on Christianity. I'm curious."

"I'm seeking, I'm praying, and I'm asking. That's where I'm at in my faith." She appeared disappointed in the lack of depth in response, so it prompted Jonathan to further explain. "I have to be honest with myself and with my faith. That's how I work as a human being. Right now, my honest truth inside my soul is how dare you, God? How dare you take the one good thing in my life? My soul was seriously wounded losing my wife."

"Oh."

Jonathan took a step closer to her. "I hope that doesn't bother you a whole lot. It's just the honest truth about where I am. My faith is lacking."

"Faith comes by hearing and hearing by the Word of God. You reading your Bible?"

He shrugged. "I should read more."

She nodded. "My faith has been a work in progress over a lot of years in my life."

Intrigued, Jonathan came another step closer. "Do you want to share with me?"

"I've lost people close to me like my friend, Betty, I've told you about. I've had to deal with being abandoned by my mother, and I had to learn to forgive an abusive ex-husband.

My faith has been small and big at moments, but God's faithfulness has always been strongest and constant throughout. It's He who delivers us through the difficulties. He carries us. Learning to trust Him isn't a matter of self-will but surrender to the truth."

"But what if you can't seem to trust Him no matter how hard you try?"

"You stop *trying*. Surrender is giving up your life and allowing Him to live through you." Her eyes went to the falls in the distance behind him. "Jesus has the living water that never runs dry. He quenches the everlasting thirst the soul has. We just have to allow Him in. Once we realize it's only He who can deliver us from ourselves, from our pains, life becomes a lot more beautiful."

CHAPTER 31

STOPPING IN OLYMPIA FOR THE night, Kylie and Jonathan unloaded the children from their car seats and let them stretch their legs for a moment in the parking lot. With the state's capital in view from the hotel parking lot, Kylie turned to Jonathan with a thankful smile. She hadn't traveled very much out of Spokane since moving there. He had opened up a whole new world to her. The Columbia River along I-84, the waterfalls in *Multnomah Falls*, and now the state's capital. Tomorrow, it'd be the ocean. She liked not only being on the road, but being with him. He was quickly becoming more than just a friend in her heart.

"I'm happy you invited me to come with you, Jonathan. A person doesn't know how much they miss out on in the world until they get a little bit of road underneath them."

He smiled warmly at her. "It's great for the body and mind to travel. I love it. I still haven't made it back east, but I hope to someday."

Kylie's eyes widened, her imagination jumping to the east coast. "Like New York City? That would be so awesome to see."

"Exactly." Opening the trunk, he grabbed their luggage, and the two of them, along with the children, headed for the hotel's front doors. Peter and Rose were holding hands with one another, and the sight of them doing so made Kylie feel warm inside. "I'm so happy they've been getting along well on this trip."

Arriving at the counter as she said it, Jonathan nodded and looked over at the two of them. "Children are amazing, aren't they? They just do. They barely think."

After he got them checked into their rooms, they headed down the hallway. Jonathan carried the luggage into the room for Kylie. The kids ran to the far side of the hotel room and began to play in the closet. The two of them watched the children for a moment. Kylie felt envious of their energy. Though she had been sitting for most of the day, she felt exhausted.

Jonathan's hand found Kylie's, surprising her and sending a welcomed chill up the length of her spine. He pulled her around the corner near the front door of the room and out of sight of the children. The way he looked into her eyes created a deep warmth in her heart. Peering into his eyes, she was overwhelmed by a sense of love wrapping around her. Then he leaned in to kiss her. A flinch flickered in her chest.

"What are you doing?" Her voice was light, not upset but gentle.

"Just doing instead of thinking." His lips curled into a smile and he came closer, lifting his hand up to her cheek. As his hand touched her cheek, she felt a shockwave ripple through her, a warm stirring in her soul. When his lips met hers, she gave in. He tasted sweet as she drank him in. Pulling his face closer to hers, she kissed him back, letting her walls down. All the worries and concerns that had once plagued her thoughts fell away in an instant.

They continued to kiss, and Jonathan slid his hands

around her waist and to the small of her back, pulling her closer to him. Her breaths became rapid, shallow between kisses. Then his lips left hers and found her neck.

She remembered the children.

Pushing him back gently, a smile still on her face, she looked at him. "We have children."

"It's probably for the better." He took a step back. "I'm not sure how good my self-control is these days." He rubbed his neck. "I'm sorry. That wasn't right to say."

Kylie stepped closer to him, resting a hand on his chest. "It's for the best that we don't."

Just then, as if God had planned it that way, Rose and Peter popped around the corner.

"Mommy, look." Peter held out his hands. Blue ink was all over his hands and Rose's too. Looking at Rose, she saw her holding a busted pen.

FINALLY IN HIS room with Rose, Jonathan shut the door. His heart was still pounding as he thought about what had just happened with Kylie. After he left her hotel room, he felt nothing but regret as he thought of only Marie. Laying Rose down in her bed to sleep, he tried to draw on his sketch pad, but his thoughts continued to drift. They would settle on Kylie for a moment, then shift like loose sand to Marie. The two women on his mind were distracting him from being able to get anything decent on the page. Frustrated, he put the sketch pad away and grabbed his ear buds and listened to his audiobook on his phone. Unable to comprehend the words being said into his ears, he stopped listening and put his phone on the nightstand. Jonathan let out a sigh, the air of turmoil escaping his lips. Then he glanced back at his phone. He couldn't help but think of Kylie's words about faith coming by hearing the Word, so he reached over and grabbed it.

He downloaded a Bible app on his phone.

Opening the app after it installed, he thumbed through the books of the Bible and randomly tapped into chapters and read. Unable to find anything that jumped off the screen, he launched a browser app on his phone and looked up Bible topics. He did searches on Scriptures related to love, joy, happiness, and then finally, grief. Each verse clicked in his mind as he looked them up on his Bible application. They made sense like he had never left the faith. But it wasn't until he arrived on a certain passage in the Psalms that he finally found a verse he felt was made for his very soul, for that very moment.

He heals the brokenhearted and binds up their wounds.
Psalm 147:3

EYES GLISTENING AND HEART ACHING, he peered up at the ceiling as he sat in his hotel room. He folded his hands and prayed. *Lord, I know I don't deserve You. I've always known that. But these last five years, I've wasted my life running away from You. It's You who can heal this pain, and I should've known that from the beginning, but I didn't.* He wiped a tear that had escaped his left eye. Jonathan's heart felt weak, his heartbeat faint. He continued praying. *I was selfish and only thinking about myself and my pain, Lord. Marie was never mine, Lord. I know that and I've always known that. She's always been Yours. Help me, Lord. Help my heart to finally heal. Your Word says You're near the brokenhearted and that's what I am. I can't run from it anymore.* Hot tears running down his cheeks, Jonathan peered over at the door of the hotel room and thought of Kylie. *Help Your will be done, Lord. Even if that means no Kylie. Amen.*

A knock came on the door. Wiping his eyes, Jonathan slipped out of bed and went to answer the door. Checking the peephole, he saw Kylie in a puddle of tears right outside in the hallway.

He opened it.

Wearing a pair of unicorn pajama pants and a hooded sweatshirt, Kylie was holding herself, her arms wrapped around her body, tears running down her cheeks and her eyes bloodshot.

"What's wrong?" His voice was a whisper. Lifting a hand, he rested it on the door frame.

Her bottom lip trembled as she brought a balled fist to her lips. "Jonathan, I like you. I like you a lot. I've fought against it since I started working for you."

"I like you too."

"No, I don't think you get what I mean." She loosed her arms, letting them fall open. "I haven't ever felt this way about someone. I'm scared. I'm scared I'll never be what Marie was to you."

His heart splintered and he dropped his hand away from the door frame. Taking a step closer, he brought his hands up to both her arms and grabbed her gently. "Why would you worry about being like Marie?"

She shrugged, more tears following. "I see the pictures around your house. You had this amazing wife and life with her, and now she's gone. I don't feel like I will *ever* be able to measure up to even a tenth of that. I mean, I'm broken and messed up and have a kid."

"Kylie . . ." Coming closer, he hugged her. "I'm messed up too, and I have a kid also. But right now, I'm trying to figure things out in my life. I'm struggling with my faith because of my wife's death. That doesn't mean I'm not over my wife. It means I'm trying to find my way back to God."

"I can't fathom what it'd be like to lose a spouse, but I think your words just now cleared some stuff up in my head. As much as I like you, I need a man who can be a father to my child and has a solid faith."

"And I can't give that to you. Not right now."

Sniffling as she took a step back, she shrugged a shoulder. "It's probably better if we part ways here?" Glancing toward her hotel door down the hall, she shook her head. "I don't think I can bear to be around you anymore, Jonathan. Especially after that kiss. That kiss did me in."

Jonathan raised an eyebrow. "What?"

"I can't be around you. Not because of anything bad but because of everything good. I love how you are, how we are on this trip, how our kids are together." She shrugged. "But I can't keep being around you and expect these feelings to stop growing."

Jonathan didn't want to force her to stay. With her permission, he pulled out his phone and booked her a flight. "Tomorrow at ten. I'll drive you two to the airport. Don't try to fight me on me being the one who is paying for it. I insist. I'm the one who made the move on you and messed everything up here."

She came in for another hug. As she walked back to her room, he shut the door gently.

CHAPTER 32

*A*FTER A QUIET DRIVE TO the airport in Olympia, Jonathan sat in the parking garage for a moment after she had gone inside with Peter to catch her flight home. He peered over at the passenger seat and felt an emptiness inside knowing Kylie wouldn't be by his side anymore. Not only on the rest of this trip, but also when he arrived home. He knew that parting ways wasn't just simply parting ways on the trip, but in life. It was the only way. Over time, he hoped they'd both be able to let go of the short romance that had sparked between them.

"Daddy." Rose's little voice carried from the back seat, calling to him for the first time with that endearment. Jonathan couldn't help but acknowledge the gift from God. His heart melted hearing Rose say 'Daddy', and he adjusted the rearview mirror to look at her. There she was, the little girl who had changed his life for the better. It was just him and her now.

He responded to her, warding off the tears. "Yes, dear?"

"Ky-ee? Pe-er?" Her palms opened wide.

"They went home, Rose."

Lowering her head, she became upset, but quietly.

He had a new problem, but he cared very little about it. There was nobody to watch Rose while he met with the client. Jonathan embraced that he was a single dad, and Nick could deal with it or find a different architect if he felt inconvenienced. Leaving Olympia, they headed toward their destination. On the road, as he put each mile behind him, he tried to forget about what had happened in Olympia with Kylie, but it wasn't easy. She had gotten beyond his walls, all his defenses. She did what no woman had been able to do since Marie had passed away. He knew he'd be okay eventually. He always found a way to push the pain down.

As the plane climbed into the sky, Kylie felt a piece of her heart was being ripped out of her chest. She had tried so hard to be careful with Jonathan, but in the end, she failed. She shouldn't have gone on the trip, shouldn't have looked at those sketches under the mattress. Nobody simply falls in love without purposely taking steps to lead themselves there. Hearing her thoughts echo the word *love* only made the hurt that much more painful. She wept quietly on the plane.

"Mommy?" Peter's concern laced his words as he gently touched her arm. She shoved the pain away from herself and forced a sad smile for her son. She had to put a brave face on and be strong for Peter.

"Mommy is okay. Everything is okay."

"You have a cute son." A man, probably in his late thirties, commented from across the aisle. His cheeky smile and fancy clothing made it apparent that he was trying to flirt with the pretty girl on the plane. She became nauseated at the thought.

"My husband and I think so." It was a lie, but it'd save her the rest of the flight from his trying to get somewhere down a road that wasn't open.

As the plane descended in Spokane a short while later, she was relieved when she turned on her phone to see her friend had come through for her. The last-minute text to Savannah before boarding their plane was received.

Savannah: Sure thing, girl. Consider me there. Need a car seat?

Savannah: Never mind, I'm bringing one anyway. My sister had her car at the restaurant so I stole hers. LOL.

Kylie grinned and joy filled her heart at the thought of Savannah being there to pick her up. A friend was exactly what she needed right now. After getting off the plane and grabbing their luggage and car seat from the luggage carousel, Peter, Kylie, and Savannah headed out of the airport.

"Wow. That's crazy. So you two broke things off because he doesn't have a strong faith?"

"I guess so. I think he's still in grief over his wife too."

"Mmmhmm . . ."

"What?" Kylie turned to Savannah with a questioning gaze.

"That man is a Penguin."

"Okay. I'm really lost now." Laughter escaped from Kylie's lips as they crossed into the parking garage.

"Penguins mate for life. Jonathan is one of those guys who only has one mate, one love. Incredibly loyal, but to a fault. Once they love, they can never love again. It's a shame. I'm sorry, girl."

Kylie mulled over her words about Jonathan. It was hard to swallow, but it was better that they were separated now. Focusing onward, she turned to her friend as they got into her car. "Can I move in with you?"

"What about your grandma?"

"I need a big change right now. Plus, your apartment is like ten minutes away. I can still visit."

"Who's going to take care of her?"

"Jenny is there."

"But isn't your grandma about to . . . you know?"

"Yes." Kylie's heart felt torn. "I'll wait a little while longer. I don't think she has much time left."

"Hm. Okay. Well, whenever you're ready."

"It'll just be temporary until I find somewhere else to work and then to live."

"Are you worried that Jonathan will come over and bug you at your grandma's?"

Kylie shook her head. "Not really. He's not that type of person. I'm more worried about myself wandering down to his door."

"Well, when you come, you'll be welcomed as long as you need." She glanced back at Peter. "And Peter can stay forever."

Laughing, Kylie smiled. "Thank you for being a true friend, Savannah."

CHAPTER 33

*M*EETING WITH TYLER ON THE beachfront property with Rose, Jonathan and he shook hands. Then Tyler took off his shades. Slipping the sunglasses in the breast pocket of his blazer, he shook his head as he looked him over from head to toe.

"You look like you didn't sleep, brother."

The wind picked up just then, blowing their clothing as they stood in the sand. Jonathan nodded. "Kylie's gone."

"What?" He opened his arms. "What did you do?"

"Nothing. Things didn't work out."

"Don't be so vague, Jonathan. What are you talking about?"

"She needs a man with a strong faith. She's a lot like Marie in that respect. I told her I'm struggling with my faith because of losing Marie, and she took that to mean I'm not over losing my wife. Regardless, I'm not the man she needs right now."

"So typical of you." Shaking his head, Tyler walked a few yards away and placed a boot up on a log as he peered out at the ocean. Jonathan soon joined him with Rose at the log. Setting her down, he turned to Tyler.

"What do you mean by that?"

He removed his foot and turned to face Jonathan. "You refuse to let yourself enjoy anything. Even when Marie was still alive, you couldn't get over the fact that she was dying and weren't able to enjoy the remainder of her life. After Marie passed away, you completely retracted and focused heavily on your work, but that didn't satisfy you either. You obsessively poured yourself into the work, and you accomplished a ton but always wanted more. Now, you get this wonderful gift from God in the form of a family, and you're too blind to even see it or enjoy it." He paused, glanced at Rose nearby, and then back at Jonathan. "It's too bad, because I would have loved to have what you just willingly threw away."

Nick showed up moments after Tyler stopped talking, and it was time to go over the concept designs. Beckoning Rose over as she was getting too far away, Jonathan introduced her as his daughter to Nick.

"I have two girls of my own." Nick smiled as his eyes stayed on Rose. "Children are a funny thing. When they're young, they are so much work, but then when they get older, like in their 20s, they're beautiful human beings if you do it right."

Jonathan was pleased to hear it mellows out in the long run. "I'm not looking forward to her being in her teenage years."

Nick laughed and waved his hands. "I wouldn't wish that on my worst enemies. But yes, children are truly a blessing."

Going over the concepts, Nick held each concept Jonathan had sketched and colored up to the spot on the beach. He wanted to see what it'd look like. Picking the third one, he nodded. "This is my casa. My whole family will come and love the beach in this house right here." He shook hands with Tyler and Jonathan, then before he left, he came closer to Jonathan. His voice was low and serious. "These little ones we are entrusted with need their dads more than anything. Have a beautiful life, Jonathan."

Nick left the beach, Tyler walking him up to his car. Jonathan turned and looked at the waves as they crashed against the shoreline. He held an uneasy feeling within him knowing that he might've just thrown away the best thing to happen in his life since Marie. He prayed. *Lord, please help me.*

THAT EVENING, instead of staying the night in Ocean Shores, Jonathan decided to drive all night in order to get home by morning. He knew sleep wasn't going to be an option for him anyway, so why not drive? It didn't take long for Rose to crash out after her chicken nuggets and milkshake. At a stop to get gas, he downloaded an audiobook of the Bible and synced his phone to his car in order to listen to it.

He spent the remainder of the trip, roughly six hours, listening to the Bible. He listened to the book of Luke and a lot of the Epistles that Paul wrote. As he listened to the same Scriptures he had heard a lifetime ago, they were emboldened with new life, new color and purpose. Things made sense now in a different light than he had previously seen them. Everything he heard was coming to life in a new way. By the time he pulled into his driveway the next morning, he shut off his car with a new perspective on life and a renewed respect for Jesus Christ.

The sun was barely coming up as he pulled a sleeping Rose from her car seat. He smiled and gently kissed her forehead. When he came back out to grab their luggage after laying Rose down, he saw Kylie's car round the corner down the street. His heart flinched.

Knowing he needed a replacement, after a much-needed nap, he spent the rest of the day on a website that was dedicated to sourcing babysitters. He found a few he liked and set up interviews with them over the course of the next few weeks. He managed to find one in particular that he really liked, and she got along well with Rose. Her name was Stephanie. She was twenty-three years old and had a year's worth of experience at a daycare. Everything was going to be okay without Kylie, at least on a working level.

CHAPTER 34

SIX WEEKS AFTER ARRIVING HOME from Olympia, Kylie went into Grandma Faith's bedroom to wake her for dinner. Walking up to the side of her bed, she gently placed a hand on her shoulder.

"It's time for dinner, Grandma."

There was no response. She checked to see if she was breathing to find she wasn't. Kylie's eyes moistened with tears and her legs weakened. Sitting down on the bed beside her, Kylie let reality set into her soul. The woman who had taught her everything she knew in life had relocated in her sleep. She was thankful that she went peacefully while napping, but it didn't make it hurt any less. Wiping her eyes, she peered up at the ceiling of the room and prayed out loud. "She's Yours now, Lord."

Jenny came in a few moments later. "The food is getting cold. What is going on?" Kylie turned to her with wet eyes and Jenny stopped her steps near the end of the bed. Frowning, she looked at Kylie. "She's gone."

Nodding, Kylie left the bed and rushed over to Jenny.

Throwing her arms around her in a warm embrace, they comforted each other in their moment of loss.

Having known that she was on her way out, Grandma Faith had prepared her exit to the utmost. She had a will in place, and the house was to be sold, the proceeds being split among the eight girls she had adopted from her years as a foster parent. She had also set apart money for a proper burial with no expense unpaid. Not only did she leave behind a legacy and her faith to the children she had raised in The Faith House, but she made sure her death wouldn't inconvenience anybody. The most shocking part of it all to Kylie was the funeral.

Droves of cars showed up for the funeral service. Hundreds of women, both young and old, showed up to pay their respects. Many took turns getting up in front of the church to share how Evelynn Faith had impacted their lives. Every person who got up to speak about her couldn't help but mention her faith in Jesus Christ. Through the tear-filled service, Kylie couldn't explain it, but she felt a yearning in her soul for Jonathan to be by her side.

She hadn't prepared or planned to say anything at the service but felt inclined toward the end to do so. Standing up, she went down the aisle and up to the pulpit where the microphone was located. Her eyes glistened with tears as she peered at the casket only a few feet away. Lifting her gaze to the audience, she could hear the faint sound of somber cries and broken hearts.

"I was one of the girls who came to The Faith House. I remember I was only seven years old when I came there. I was troubled and unloved when I showed up on that doorstep, but she loved me anyway. When I left The Faith House years later to marry my first husband, I remember her warning me about him. She was right, like she always tended to be. But you know what? She still took me back in. My relationship with Grandma Faith reminds me so much of our relationship, or my relationship more specifically, with the Lord. We accept, we love, and then we run away and do our own thing. Then we come back and feel like an idiot, but He is there waiting for us and still loving us." Kylie paused, dabbing her eyes with a tissue from the pulpit. "Grandma Faith taught me everything I know, and even though she's gone now, she's left so much love behind. She changed my life forever by introducing me to God-sized love, and I'm eternally thankful for her. If it wasn't for her, I'd be on my way to Hell, I'm sure of it." Her eyes fell to the casket a few feet away. With tears in her eyes and a cracking voice, she said, "I love you, Mom."

CHAPTER 35

ON HER DRIVE TO WORK at *Petco* a little over a year later, Kylie was praying and thinking about how blessed she was in life. She was only months away from completing her college courses and had already put in an application to a local Christian school in Spokane. They weren't hiring right now, but they said they would keep her resume on file. Her job at *Petco* had been going great and she was even promoted a few months back for her hard work and drive that she showed in the store. Peter was growing a little more every day, and she was too.

Suddenly, her phone rang.

It was an unknown but local number. She knew it could be the school, but more realistically, it was probably the apartment complex she had submitted an application to a week ago. She answered the call.

"This Kylie Hawthorne?"

"It is."

"Great. This is Chantel with Saddlewood Apartments. I have a question about your application, if you have a moment."

"Okay, go ahead." Kylie pulled into the parking lot of *Petco* and parked in a parking stall in the back row.

"Did whoever showed you the apartment go over the move-in costs to live here?"

"Yes, first and last month's rent with a $600 deposit."

"Yep. That's it."

"So I got the apartment?"

"Yes!"

"Yay!" Kylie's eyes glistened with tears of joy. "Thank you so much!"

Hanging up with the apartment manager, relief overwhelmed her and she thanked God in prayer. She loved living with Savannah, but it had been difficult sharing a home with her. Peter was getting more active by the day and needed a place of his own to move about freely. This would be the perfect place to live for the two of them, and it was only a block away from his daycare.

AFTER WORK and picking up Peter, she got home and broke the news to Savannah. They danced around in circles, then sat down on the couch.

"You're finishing up your degree in Early Childhood Education next month, have a new place to live, and recently got a promotion at work. How could life get any better?" Savannah's question was rhetorical, but that didn't stop a certain person from entering her mind. Jonathan still came up often in her mind, almost daily. Her feelings for him had dulled over time, but they were still there. She wondered if he had found God again and if he had finally moved on from Marie. She wondered about Rose too. She had grown close to her in her time employed by Jonathan. Something in

Kylie's face must have shifted when she thought of him because it prompted Savannah to ask, "What's wrong, girl?"

Kylie hesitated. Her heart pounded at the thought of bringing him up. She couldn't hide the truth. She wasn't able to fully enjoy this victory, or any of them, without thinking about the man who had stolen her heart over a year ago on a trip to the ocean. She caved in. "It's *Jonathan*." Her eyes glistened at merely saying the name. "I still think about him often. I can't seem to dislodge him from my heart."

Savannah was quiet for a moment, then she folded her hands in her lap. Concerned, she tilted her head. "How long has it been now?"

"A little over a year."

Scooting closer, she put a hand on Kylie's back. "Can I pray with you over this?"

"Yes, please." She wiped her eyes and bowed her head along with Savannah.

"Lord, we come to Your throne right now and ask You to show Kylie it's You alone who can bring us happiness. It's You alone who can complete us. We ask right now, Lord, that You put Your arms around Kylie's heart and hold her. Just hold her and show her Your powerful and everlasting love made possible through Jesus Christ. We ask these things in Your Holy and Precious name, Jesus. Amen."

Wiping a stray tear, Kylie thanked Savannah and gave her a hug. Peter came up to her a moment later with a race car in his hand. It was a welcomed interruption by her little guy.

"I love you, Mommy."

Smoothing her hand over the top of Peter's head, she smiled warmly at him. "I love you too, dear."

CHAPTER 36

*A*RRIVING TO THE CALVARY CHAPEL Jonathan had been attending for almost a year and a half now, he grabbed his Bible from the front passenger seat and headed through the double doors that led into the church. This morning was his weekly men's Bible study he had been attending for the last eleven months. Through reading his Bible daily, praying, and attending services whenever the doors were opened, Jonathan had not only rediscovered his love for the Lord but had gone deeper than ever before. Once inside, Tom, one of the church associate pastors, stopped him.

"Good morning, John. Beautiful day God has given us, isn't it?"

"Morning, Tom. It sure is."

Entering the fellowship hall, the old sanctuary now used for Bible studies and children's ministry worship, he set his Bible down on one of the metal tables. He proceeded over to the coffee and donuts on a table. He grabbed a cup and turned the knob on the coffee to fill his cup. Just then,

Howard, the leader of his Tuesday night Bible study group, approached him.

Jonathan turned toward him and smiled. "How are you doing, brother?"

"I'm great." He stopped and they exchanged handshakes before he continued. "Kenny over at the school said you're trying to get your daughter enrolled in preschool over there?"

Jonathan had been in talks with Pastor Gedstead, the pastor of Calvary Chapel, for months in the hopes of getting Rose enrolled in the school on the church campus. The issue was the fact that all the school rosters were full and his hands were tied at the present time.

"Yeah, I'd love to get her in, but there just isn't much they can do with full classes."

He nodded. "I'll see what I can do about that. I'll be praying for you, bud. Lord loves you." Howard patted his shoulder and headed over to talk to other men who were arriving. Each person he came near, he greeted and hugged.

A smile on his face and inside his heart, Jonathan took his coffee and sat down at the table with his Bible on it. The Lord had been working in Jonathan's life in a major way lately. He had discovered the beauty in the true surrender of his life to His Savior, Jesus Christ. His life was not his own, but Jesus's. He had no control, no power, and no reliance on any one person except Jesus.

It was through learning these truths that Jonathan was able to fully return to his faith and embrace the reality that Marie was never his, but the Lord's. All his anger and resentment fell away from him like an old layer of skin falling off after a sunburn. Piece by piece, day by day, the old nature flaked off, revealing his new regenerated self in Jesus. Though he had come to these conclusions about Jesus, about Marie, he hadn't pursued a relationship with Kylie. He had done some light research on Social Media and discovered she was doing well and appeared to have moved on. He prayed for her and Peter's safety and wellbeing daily, but he felt it was better if he left the two of them alone.

Michael, the men's Bible study leader, caught everyone's attention a few minutes after eight o'clock and requested they all stand while they sang worship songs to God. As Jonathan sang, he raised his hands in the air and focused his heart on Jesus. He was by no means an excellent singer, but that didn't stop him. He knew that God didn't care about his lack of talent in singing but looked at his heart.

After singing, all the men present, about sixteen in total, pushed the tables together to form a square in the center of the room. It was time to study the Word of God. They opened in prayer and then turned to Matthew chapter six. They read a few verses, then stopped and discussed amongst the group. Then, they arrived to a passage that spoke to Jonathan's heart, convicting him.

For if you forgive other people when they sin against you, your heavenly Father will also forgive you.
But if you do not forgive others their sins, your Father will not forgive your sins.
Matthew 6:14-15

MICHAEL PAUSED AFTER READING. Surveying the men in the group, his eyes stopped on Jonathan. "What say you, Jonathan?"

His heart pounded as that day at Marie's wake pressed against his mind. The hurt, the pain, the words. He could see with absolute clarity his father in-law's disgust as he blamed

Jonathan for Marie's untimely death. Jonathan swallowed, trying to shove the memory down and away from his mind. He knew he couldn't hide from that day, from the pain. "We have to forgive. It's a lot easier to say and think about than actually do. Honestly, right now, I'm thinking about the one person in my life I never forgave."

Jonathan felt comfortable with these men around him. He could freely share without worry of condemnation.

Howard raised his hand as the silence invaded for a second in the group. Michael nodded to him to speak. "I think forgiveness is simply a matter of a change of mind. The only time we withhold forgiveness is when we're not thinking about the forgiveness Jesus Christ extended to us. He literally died for us, and on an individual and personal level, He did this. We did wrong in the sight of God and are forgiven of *everything*. With that in mind, we should be equipped to truly forgive people when we keep hold of the truth of how much we have been forgiven."

More people spoke up and tossed in their experiences and ideas, but Jonathan retracted into himself as he mulled over Howard's comment about forgiveness. Everything he had said was true. There was no denying that. Then, knowing it was right, Jonathan let go of his father-in-law's wrongdoing and truly forgave him. The weight of the burden immediately lifted from his heart as Jonathan took it to the cross and gave it over to God.

After the men's Bible study, he got into his car with the overwhelming desire to see his father-in-law. It had been six years. Jonathan wanted to hug him and let him know he had forgiven him. With his father-in-law being a pastor and the time it had been since Marie's death, he felt it was a swell idea. Leaving the parking lot of the church, he drove over to Tyler's house.

"You're just going to go? What about your house? Your fish?"

"My fish?" Jonathan leaned forward and laughed. "Can you feed them while I'm gone? You have a key. It's only three hours away. I doubt I'll be staying for very long. Maybe I'll drive home in the morning or something."

"I guess I can feed them." Tyler laughed. Then, he began to pace in his living room. Then he turned to Jonathan. "People don't do this. They don't just jump in their cars and go to someone's house who, A, hates you and, B, hasn't seen you in six years."

Jonathan laughed, joy rising up within him. "I know it's crazy, but I feel like I need to, and really, I miss the guy. I have his granddaughter, for crying out loud."

He shrugged, opening his palms out. "Okay. Take care. You want me to watch Rose for you?"

Glancing over at Rose, he shook his head. "No, I think he'd like to meet her."

Leaving his brother's house, he headed to Missoula, Montana to see the man who had crushed his spirit on that grimly cold and rainy day at the wake for Marie. He had entertained the thought of the drive for years, but not with the intent of hugging him and letting him know he had forgiven him. Something had moved deeply within Jonathan that morning at the men's Bible study. Not only was there guilt over his non-forgiveness, but the love and sadness he felt for his father-in-law. He wanted to stand face-to-face with the man who had caused him so much pain and experience how it felt not to hold that pain he had held onto for so long.

CHAPTER 37

*P*ULLING INTO THE DRIVEWAY, JONATHAN followed the gravel road over a bridge and up a slanted hill to a farmhouse. Unsure of what to expect, he left Rose in the car with the Christian radio station on, telling her he had to see someone really quick and then they'd go get a Happy Meal. Jonathan stood at the bumper, waiting for his father-in-law to realize he was there and to come out from the house. His heart pounded as different emotions tied to a series of scenarios played out in his mind.

Mr. Gillshock walked out from the farmhouse's side door off the patio with a cane. He made his way out toward Jonathan in the driveway. The man kept his eyes down and his cane moving. Each step he came closer to Jonathan caused the well of emotions from the past to stir within him. He had a long history with the man, none of it good, none of it easy to think about for Jonathan.

"Pastor." Jonathan's greeting was soft, with respect, just like when he was a boy all those years ago in high school.

Stopping short of Jonathan, he peered past him and into

183

the car. He didn't speak, just looked, then his gaze landed on Jonathan.

Tossing a nervous thumb toward the car, Jonathan forced himself to smile. "That's your granddaughter, Rose. Thought you might want to meet her."

"What are you doing here?"

"I came to see you. To let you know I forgive you for what you said all those years ago."

He squinted, his face twisting into a grimace. "You came to forgive me? You have some nerve showing up here, boy. I know what you did to my daughter, Shawna. You took her daughter from her just like you took Marie's life. You're a selfish jerk who only thinks of himself, and you think everything is okay because you say a little prayer at night. You've destroyed my family."

Jonathan's heartbeat picked up tempo, his disappointment rising up within him like a violent sea. "Dan, she left her kid with me."

"Yes, temporarily, and you went ahead and took her daughter away from her by getting guardianship."

"You could've done something about it. You didn't even show up at the court date, Dan."

"I wasn't moved to do anything about it at the time."

"But you're moved to tell me how to run my life? Are you kidding?"

"Get off my property. I never want to speak to you or see you again."

Jonathan returned to his driver side door as disbelief overtook him. He got back into his car. Watching his father-in-law through the windshield as he wobbled back into his house, Jonathan felt sadness for the man who claimed to be a man of God.

"Time for food, Daddy?"

"Yes, dear."

Looking once more to the house, Jonathan pulled out of the driveway for the last time. All that hatred in his heart was not from God, but from the depths of hell itself.

On the drive back to Spokane, Jonathan thought about the exchange between himself and his father-in-law. Though he had driven a little more than three hours out of his way to go speak with the man for a three-second conversation, Jonathan felt good that he had made the drive. He knew now that the issue didn't reside within himself, but with Dan. Dan had a corrupted heart that had been twisted and distorted, not by God but by the cares of this world. Jonathan prayed with tear-filled eyes that God could reach his father-in-law.

ARRIVING HOME, Jonathan checked the messages on his cell phone after plugging it in to charge. There was a message from Pastor Gedstead. Listening to it, he set his keys on the counter and pulled out a cup from the cupboard.

"Hey, Jonathan. It's me, Pastor. I wanted to let you know those prayers of yours worked. I spoke with the principal and the admissions counselor today at the church, and it turns out they just had a boy move away from the area in Mrs. Riley's pre-school class. You're in. Give me a call back and we can go over some details."

Jonathan jumped as he sprinted into the living room. Scooping Rose up, he twirled her around. "You're going to school!"

"Really? What about Stephanie? Will she go with me?"

He smiled. "No, you'll be in pre-school now. You'll go be with other kids, just like at church, and you'll learn about God and the alphabet, and shapes and colors and all that good stuff!"

"But I love Stephanie." Rose was somber. She didn't

understand the good news as fully as Jonathan did. He set her down and smoothed his hand over her hair as he knelt down and met her at eye level.

"I know, but this is a good thing, honey. You're going to love it."

"Are you sure, Daddy?"

His heart smiled, matching his lips. "Yes, I'm sure."

They hugged.

∿

AFTER DINNER and putting Rose down for the night, Jonathan went and worked out. As he walked out of the bathroom after his shower, he toweled his hair. Seeing the notebook sticking out from under the mattress, he thought of his past hurts and his personal history. He had used that notebook to journal his feelings through pictures and drawings. He thought of Kylie and their trip together too. He had slipped his sketches from the falls in there when he arrived home from Ocean Shores. His heart ached. He regretted much of his life after losing Marie, but he regretted Kylie most of all. From time to time, when she came to his mind, he'd pray for her, and then he'd ask himself the most terrible question. *What if he'd tried to stop her from getting on the plane that day?*

CHAPTER 38

SHORTLY AFTER MOVING INTO HER apartment with Peter, Kylie heard back on the application she had submitted months ago to the Christian school. They didn't have anything in teaching at the moment, but they did have a need for a teacher's aide. She interviewed a few days after the call and was extended an offer for the position a week later. It'd be a slight pay decrease, but she'd end up ahead financially with free childcare for her son. After accepting the job, she turned in her notice at *Petco* without a bit of hesitation. Another victory, another time of thinking about Jonathan.

Her first day on the job consisted of shadowing the other teacher's aide who had been covering both the upper and lower grades for the school. The woman she was shadowing was named Crystal, and she came across to Kylie as a resilient and marvelous woman of God.

Walking down the hardwood floored hallway quickly, Kylie fell slightly behind Crystal in the hall. Crystal glanced back at her. "Your feet will get use to moving. You do a lot of that here."

Suddenly stopping, Crystal turned and shoved a key into a side door and let Kylie enter in first. Following behind, she let the door close.

"What's this?" Kylie's eyes surveyed the room. It held a small desk, an industrial-size printer, and a large laminating machine.

"This is the resource room. Basically your home base, or when the kids are being crazy, your sanctuary away from the chaos. I eat my lunch in here most days. You can do the same if you wish. The only thing I ask is if you take a soda from the fridge, you replace it or get on the list."

"List?"

"Yes. We have a list of teachers and teacher's aides who all take turns buying cases of soda." Pausing, Crystal checked her watch. "We have kindergarten lunch in five minutes. Let's roll."

Leaving the resource room, Crystal led her to the lunchroom in the fellowship hall. As they entered, Crystal turned to her and lowered her voice as she came close. "Don't let these kindergartners fool you with their cute smiles and adorable outfits. They're ruthless, and if they sense a weakness or smell a lack of confidence, they'll tear you to shreds. You've been warned."

Suddenly, she reached a hand out, stopping a small boy from throwing a milk. She set it down on the table and turned her head toward the child sternly but with love.

"You know better than that, Landan."

Crystal continued showing and explaining to Kylie the ins and outs of the school. As they walked past the preschool doors, Crystal pointed them out. "Those are the preschool rooms. They have their own individual aides who work inside each classroom from time to time, so you won't be dealing with them at all." Kylie glanced at the closed doors and kept following.

~

JONATHAN WAS nervous when Tuesday morning finally came and it was time to drop Rose off to pre-school at Calvary Chapel. He dressed her up in a red dress with white flowers spotted all over. She also had a plastic red flower in her hair, just above her ear. Bending a knee in the hallway outside her class, he looked her over once, twice, and a third time. Jonathan was sure that he was far more nervous about her going to school for the first time than she was. She was eager to join the other kids filing in through the doorway, her eyes darting at the kids as each one passed through the doorway.

"Daddy," Rose whined, pulling from his hold toward the doorway. "I want to go in."

His eyes glistened and he fought tears. "You going to be okay all day alone? Do you want to go to home and I'll let Stephanie know you're not doing school?" He immediately regretted his words. He stood up and nodded, telling himself and Rose that everything would be okay. "You'll be fine. *We* will be fine."

Leading her inside the classroom, he surveyed the room, taking everything in while at the same moment, searching for the teacher. He saw a woman in a dress standing near a desk. "Let's go meet Mrs. Riley." Walking with Rose by his side, they went over and introduced themselves to each other. After speaking with her teacher for a moment, he felt better about Rose being at school and he was finally able to peel himself away as he saw her jumping into the block action a few of the kids were involved in on the other side of the room.

In the hallway, he walked down the smooth hardwood floors, thinking of Rose as he did. Turning his head, he glanced back at the classroom, not realizing he was walking directly into someone. Crash, a stack of papers fell to the floor. Embarrassed but respectful, he started to help pick them up. "I'm so sorry. Oh, Crystal! Good to see you again."

"Hey, Jonathan! It's been awhile. Are you still going on Tuesday nights? I haven't been going to the Bible study lately because of a ladies' group that started up."

"Ahh, I wondered about you and your husband. That's good you're still plugged in though."

"Absolutely. I'd better keep moving. It was nice seeing you."

"You too. Bye."

They went their separate ways. As Jonathan walked, he thought of Rose, even worried about her. He hoped in his heart that her first day would be enjoyable for her.

CHAPTER 39

A FEW DAYS LATER, KYLIE was set free to be on her own. She had her name badge, keys, and whistle all hanging from a lanyard that hung around her neck. Arriving ten minutes early to the school, she went into the school office to say hello to her new friend Elizabeth at the receptionist counter. They fell into a light conversation about an upcoming field trip when the principal, and Kylie's boss, Tanya, walked into the office.

"Good. You're already here, Kylie. Come with me."

Kylie followed Tanya into her office as she threw her purse onto a chair near the office window and flipped on a light switch. "I know it's a big favor to ask, but you said you really wanted to be a teacher in your interview."

Kylie's heart began to pound. "Yes. That's correct."

"Mrs. Riley is out sick today. Her son Gregory was up all night ill. It's only preschool, so I figured I'd give you a shot if you wanted it. It's not as intense of a curriculum like the higher grades. As you know, your son, Peter, is in the other preschool class, so it's not going to be a distraction to have Mommy teaching. You up for it?"

"I'll do it." Her heart was racing now. "I'm scared to death, but I'll do it!"

Tanya came over to Kylie and tilted her head, smiling. "You'll do great, and know we're all praying for you. Head to Mrs. Riley's and get ready for parents."

Smiling as she left the office and headed to her classroom, she thanked God over and over for the chance to finally be a teacher. Sure, it was four year olds, but it was a chance to do what she had envisioned herself doing for years. Coming into the classroom, she turned on the light. The walls were decorated in all sorts of nature scenes and bugs. Butterflies, ladybugs and grasshoppers about filled every square inch of the classroom. There were also shrubbery and trees, along with a chore calendar and days of the week. Her eyes glistened with tears of happiness as she thought about all those kids relying on her to teach them. She thought of her Grandma Faith and her heart warmed knowing she'd be proud of her. Realizing she needed to find a lesson plan quickly, Kylie began to search the counters, drawers, and cupboards.

Crystal opened the door and walked in with a packet in hand.

"Need this?" she asked, smiling as she walked over to Kylie.

Kylie's tensed muscles relaxed seeing that her entire day was laid out before her on an 8 x 9 piece of paper. "I created these for occasions like this. Emergency lesson plans for substitutes."

"You really like your job, don't you?"

"I love it. Text me if you need anything or run into issues." Stopping at the door with her hand on the door handle, Crystal turned and looked at Kylie. "You're going to rock it today, girl. Praying for you."

Crystal left, but before the door shut behind her, a man's

hand stopped it. Pulling the door open, the man entered the classroom.

Seeing who it was, Kylie's heart jolted.

"Jonathan?"

He didn't say anything but just held onto Rose's hand as she attempted to sprint. Then he let go, and she ran to Kylie, wrapping her arms around her legs.

"Kylie!"

Her heart melted that Rose had remembered who she was. Overwhelmed, she couldn't speak as more parents and children showed up.

Jonathan panicked and said, "I got to go."

"Me too. Um, I mean, I have to teach." Her heart was pounding so hard she was barely able to think. Her throat was closed up tight as it felt like someone had choked her. She couldn't believe he was there, right in front of her. Then, before she could even blink a few times, he was gone out the door. With him out of sight, her heartbeat settled down and she was able to compose herself. Everything felt fine, as long as she didn't look at Rose for too long.

JONATHAN PACED in circles outside the classroom as he debated on what to do. He wanted to go in there and pull her out of class to talk to her, to confess that he'd never stopped loving her. But he rejected the notion right away. He couldn't rip her from her classroom. Then he thought, *she must have a boyfriend. Maybe she didn't publicize it on Facebook or something. She looked amazing. She looked happy. And that, Mr. Dunken, had nothing to do with you! Once you showed up, she became miserable instantly! You saw her face!*

"Jonathan." Pastor Gedstead approached with open arms,

walking toward him in the hallway. "What's going on? You look a little beside yourself."

He stopped pacing. Once he stopped moving, his eyes glistened as he felt his heart aching in a deep way. It had been so long since he had seen her, but the feelings weren't even dulled a little, like he had thought they were. If anything, they were stronger than the day she left on that airplane in Olympia. "The woman filling in for Mrs. Riley is the woman I love."

The pastor's eyes widened. "The one that got away?"

"The one that got away." Jonathan's eyes fixed on the door a few feet away. "She was gone, man. I thought I was getting over her. It's been a year and a half since I saw her last." He shook his head, his gaze falling back on the pastor. "I love her still like the day I let her go. She must be married or dating now. She looked too happy to not have someone."

Suddenly, Crystal came hurrying down to the door of Kylie's classroom and went inside.

Jonathan lowered his head. He now knew she wasn't doing well at all after seeing him. He had brought it on.

"I have to go, Pastor. I'll see you around. Okay?"

"Okay. But before you go, can I pray with you?"

"Sure."

Lowering their heads together, the pastor placed his hand on Jonathan's shoulder and led a short prayer. "Father, God, Your ways are above our ways. You have absolute and perfect wisdom in all situations that go on in our lives. Help give us the peace that only You can offer. Please, Lord, whatever Jonathan is going through right now, I ask that You help him. Amen."

"Thank you." Jonathan smiled warmly at the pastor.

"Take care, brother, and have an excellent day."

CHAPTER 40

WHEN KYLIE'S LUNCH BREAK CAME, she hurried her steps down the hall and to the resource room. Today, it was a sanctuary, not from the children but from her heartache. Her eyes buried in the palms of her hands, she cried out in prayer, asking God, *'Why, God? Why does he have to have Rose go here?'*

The door opened, and it was Crystal. She was such a kind soul. After getting her text for a five-minute break right after seeing Jonathan, she showed up and jumped in with no questions asked. Kylie made her way to the bathroom and composed herself and returned to class. Crystal shut the door of the resource room behind her and approached with concern and love in her eyes. She sat down across from Kylie.

"Do you want to talk about it?"

Letting out a heavy sigh, Kylie wiped under her eyes with her fingertips. "What is there to talk about? I fell in love with a man who couldn't be what I needed. He still loved his deceased wife at the time and didn't have a love of or for God. I left my job working for him and I hadn't seen him in a year and a half. But for some silly reason, I still have feelings for the man. I just want the pain to stop, you know? I don't like the knot in my chest."

Crystal listened as Kylie went on to fill her in about a few details of hers and Jonathan's history. She told her about how things had started simple and then about their trip with the kids. Then, ultimately, how things became real and ended after they shared a kiss in her hotel room. She revealed and opened up about it all. This reason might have been the sheer fact that Crystal was just the only one there, but Kylie felt it was more than that. Kylie had taken a liking to Crystal from the very moment they had met.

"Hey. It just dawned on me. I know Jonathan. He was in my Bible study back a while ago. He seemed like a good guy with an authentic faith."

Kylie raised an eyebrow. "That's good to hear. It's just all hard to understand. You know?"

Crystal nodded and moved a chair, positioning it beside Kylie. "Can I tell you something about me?"

"Yes, please do."

"My father was killed a couple of years ago. Some stranger just shot him on a random California boardwalk. There was no reason for the death. It wasn't even an accident or because someone didn't like him. It just happened." She paused, dabbing her eyes with her thumbs as she stirred up the pain.

"How are you so bubbly and happy in life with that fact looming?"

"Believe me, I wasn't at first. I was very upset, and it was toward God for allowing something like that to happen. I was so angry, Kylie. But it was because I was focused on myself and my pain. Once I pressed into God and let myself fall deeper in love with my Creator, I realized something. This life is fleeting. God doesn't cause the pains in our life, but He can teach us from them. I've never walked so closely to God as I do now, and it only happened after losing my dad. He was a great father for that period of time that he was one, but now he's gone, and that's okay."

Kylie breathed deeply, letting her muscles relax along with her stirring emotions. She thought of Grandma Faith. "I recently lost the closest thing to a mother I had growing up. It was easier than I thought it would be to let her go since I knew it was coming, but there was a peace with it."

Crystal nodded. "When there's a secure faith in a person, letting go of a loved one can be easier. You know, the fact that Jonathan is bringing Rose to this school should be a good sign to you. From what you told me about his lack of faith and the fact that I knew him from Bible study? All good signs."

"Thank you." Reaching out, she touched Crystal's hand. "And thanks for taking the time to talk to me."

"You're welcome."

JONATHAN THANKED Tyler on the phone for agreeing to pick up Rose for him at the school. He was in his studio working on a new building re-design of an old decrepit warehouse downtown. A super-rich twenty-year-old wanted to turn the historic eyesore into a new tech startup headquarters.

The front door chimed, and he set his pencil down on the desk. Walking out from his studio, he went to answer it. As he opened the door, he said, "Did you forget you have a key?"

Tyler laughed. "No. I just like making you walk."

He let go of Rose's hand as Jonathan bent down, and she leapt into his arms.

"Daddy! I loved school with Kylie!"

"Good, honey. Tell me all about it."

They walked through the foyer toward the living room, listening to Rose talk about her time with Kylie. Once in the living room, Tyler and Jonathan sat down on the couch while Rose got busy pulling out her toys from the toy box beside the TV.

Jonathan turned to his brother. "What'd she say?"

"Not much more than a friendly 'hello.'"

Adjusting on the couch, Jonathan got on the edge of his cushion. "What else? How'd she seem?"

"Like a teacher?" He laughed. "I don't know, man. If you care so much, you should've gone and talked to her."

Shoving a hand through the air, Jonathan stood up. "I just need to know how she feels, what she's thinking. You know?"

"You've got to go get her then, man. If you really care, you can't hide in your house and hope she comes crawling."

Wiping his face, Jonathan nodded, then turned. "Wait. What if she rejects me?"

"Then you move on." Tyler stood, patting his shoulder. "You know what, brother? You weren't ready for that woman when she came into your life. You were a God-hating, workaholic, angry and cold man who had no friends besides me, and that's because I have to love you. The way God used Rose's coming here still baffles me to this day. You were a rock that was impenetrable, and God got through to you with this little girl who calls you Daddy. Now it's time to go get your woman."

CHAPTER 41

*A*FTER THE CHILDREN LEFT FOR the day, there was a bit of cleanup left for Kylie in Mrs. Riley's classroom. She had successfully made it through the day, despite the train wreck of emotions that showed up first thing in the morning in her classroom's doorway. Her nerves were settled now, and she had been relieved to see that Tyler instead of Jonathan had come to pick up Rose in the afternoon. She loved seeing Rose again during class, this time as her teacher. It was a painfully sweet reminder of their time together at Jonathan's house.

A rapping of knuckles lightly knocked on the door, then it opened.

Kylie turned to see who it was.

It was Crystal. She walked in. Her mouth tipped into a smile as she raised an eyebrow on her approach. "How'd it go the rest of the day?" Her voice was sympathetic, her demeanor understanding and caring. "Hopefully, it wasn't too bad."

"Our talk earlier helped a lot. Thanks again for that." Reaching over to the floor, Kylie picked up a pile of blocks that Nathaniel, one of her students, had left behind from his playtime after nap. She dropped them into the crate beside her and lifted her gaze to Crystal. "Why'd it have to work out like this, I wonder? His daughter goes here? What kind of weird coincidence is that?"

Crystal shrugged. "Maybe it's not a coincidence. Maybe it's God's way of nudging you. I don't want to put words into God's mouth, but look at it. You get hired on here and then you, on a freak whim, substitute in his daughter's class? Either tell him how you feel or forget about him and move on, honey." After a few seconds, Kylie heard Crystal's footsteps leave the classroom.

Kylie walked over to the counter with a sink in it and grabbed the yellow sponge to clean up the marker that had made its way onto one of the tables. Leaning over, she wiped away the blue and red marks and whispered to herself. "I can't forget him because I love him."

Turning her head back to the task at hand, a sparkle caught her eye on the table next to the one she was cleaning.

There was a ring.

Confusion filled her as she walked over to the table. She lifted the ring from the table and looked at it.

"I love you too."

Her heart pounded as her gaze lifted from the ring to see Jonathan in the doorway of the classroom.

"Jonathan." Her voice was a soft whisper, and she could feel tingles chasing the length of her spine as she felt frozen in time. He walked between the children's tables and gently took the ring from her and slipped it onto her finger.

"Think about it. I know I have." Moving past her, he went to the other table where the sponge was and picked it up. Kylie said nothing but cleaned too. They worked together to clean the mess of the room left by the little angels she had taught. Jonathan wiped everything down while Kylie put craft supplies back into their proper places. By the end of it, the room shined and looked to be in order.

Walking out of the room with Jonathan, Kylie flipped the light switch off.

Once in the hall, Jonathan stopped and turned to her. "I don't even know if you're dating someone or married, but I hope not. I can't ignore what happened this morning. I felt something, the same something I felt way back in Olympia so long ago. I thought my feelings for you were dulling and going away, but when I saw you . . . it all came rushing back to me, stronger than ever."

Kylie's heart pounded. She felt scared as she looked at the ring on her finger. "I've thought of you too, Jonathan."

Seeing a few teachers walking down the hallway, Kylie motioned for Jonathan to continue with her down the hall to the room where Peter was located, in after-school daycare.

"Just a second." Entering the room, Kylie saw Peter playing with cars on a track on the other side of the large stretched room. Walking over to him, she watched as he shared the red car in his hand with the boy who was sitting there. She smiled, her heart melting at the kindness of her son. Scooping him up, she left the room and returned to Jonathan in the hallway.

JONATHAN SMILED at Peter and said hello. He hid his eyes in his mother's shoulder. She covered the back of his head, smoothing her hand gently over his hair. "He's just a little shy."

It stung Jonathan knowing that Peter had forgotten who he was. He began to worry. She still hadn't responded to the ring, yet she was wearing it. His eyes went to the ring, and she shifted her gaze to the hall.

They walked out of the school and to her parked car under a white willow tree. She strapped Peter in his car seat in the back of her car, and as she came out, he felt the time dwindling. He touched her arm, stepping closer to her as she shut the back door.

"So tell me. What do you say?" Jonathan didn't want to ask if the answer was 'yes,' but he surely couldn't leave and part ways without hearing an answer.

Her eyes fell away from him, stirring more worry in Jonathan. Her gaze came back to him. "Jonathan, I haven't been able to get you out of my mind since the day I stepped onto that airplane. I didn't like what happened in Olympia. The kiss, the parting we had. But it had to be for a reason."

He gently pulled her hand into his and kissed the top of it. Letting it down slowly, he shook his head, his gaze still on her. "I learned a whole lot while we have been apart. It had to be that way in order for God to do His work in me, have me love Him first. I came to realize I had loved Marie more than I had loved God. But I have grown spiritually since then, and God is my Lord and Savior and He will always be first in my life. Kylie, I loved having you in my life every day. Before you and Rose came into my life, I was miserable. You didn't save me or lead me directly back to God, but you played a big part in my being open to it. I love you."

"You love Marie still." He tilted his head, a smile beaming from his lips.

"She will always be in my heart, but she is in Heaven and my love for her isn't the same as when she was on Earth. God showed me that. I had to love God in a pure and true way first before He led me back to you. I found my reason to live, not in you, but in God through a real and authentic relationship with Jesus. That wouldn't have happened if it wasn't for Rose coming to live with me. It wouldn't have happened without your showing up on my doorstep the Monday after I offered you the job at your old job at *Ethan's*."

With tears in her eyes, she lunged forward and wrapped her arms around Jonathan.

"Yes. I will marry you!"

They kissed. As Jonathan deepened the kiss beneath the willow tree, a few of the leaves began to tumble atop their heads, but they paid no attention. They had found a love that they both knew they could cherish for a lifetime. A love that was a friendship at first, an explosion a little while later, and then deepened by their faith in Christ.

The End.

Continue reading "A Reason To Love" series… Book 2, "A Reason To Believe"

Prologue

THE FIRST TIME I LAID eyes on Kirk was back in our senior year of High School while I was walking the track with Chloe. He was beneath the bleachers lip-locked with Vicky Haggar from the cheerleading squad. This wouldn't have been an issue outside of the fact that he was dating my best-friend, Chloe. Not exactly a best first impression.

Two years later when I was twenty, I decided to relocate from Albany, New York, to Spokane, Washington. Kirk had found out about the big journey across country through mutual friends and approached me about road tripping together. I quickly rejected him. When he offered to pay for all the gas, I couldn't help but give in. With over 2,000 miles to reach Spokane and a strong desire not to rely on my parents anymore, I knew his gas money would help me in the long run. I was on my way to Spokane to stake a claim in my independence from my parents and to work at a software company as a receptionist. Kirk had been into hockey and hoped for a chance at the big leagues by trying out for the Spokane Chiefs.

Through the long journey across the country, somewhere between Buffalo and Cleveland, I suspect, Kirk and I became friends. During our time together on the road, we laughed about Mrs. Bovey, our ninth-grade English teacher who hated children far too much to be teaching them in a school. We also shared our hopes and desires for the future.

When we finally arrived in Spokane five days after we left our hometown, I not only had a handful of memories from our road trip but a longing for something more for *us*. The trip had given me a chance to see past the façade he had put on in high school and see the real Kirk. At one stop along the way, at a gas station out in the middle of nowhere, he opened my car door for me. Then another time, he grabbed me my favorite candy bar without my even having to ask. When I became tired of driving, he'd willingly take over even if he was tired. Beyond those sweet gestures, I learned of a man who held a lot of regret over his checkered past. He had high hopes to start afresh and make a new life for himself in Spokane. Beneath all the muscles, I found a man with a big heart.

I couldn't give into my desire to see him again, though, or to possibly have a relationship. He was, after all, Chloe's ex-boyfriend. I dropped him off at the bus stop where his friend was picking him up and said goodbye for what I thought was forever.

Chapter 1-Jessica

FIVE YEARS AND TWO JOBS later, I was on my way to work when I stopped in at a favorite local coffee shop of mine downtown, Milo's, for an extra boost of caffeine. I had already been running late for work as it was, sleeping through all three of my alarms. There was a reason to the madness. It was all due to my friend Isabella, who had kept me up half the night on the phone. She was like me, single and living on the hopes of someday being swept away by a gallant gentleman who would show us the love we needed. We talked last night about how miserable she was being single in a world full of married men, the only single ones being creeps. I understood the pain of loneliness, but only to a certain degree. My singleness was part of who I was. It had almost become a friend. Sure, I wanted someone to love and hold, but I had to trust the fact that God was in control and knew my heart. Plus, I had my work, which filled much of my time.

Standing in the coffee shop near the counter, I waited for my order. I had on my new white pea coat I had just picked up the other day at the mall. When I saw it hanging on the rack on my way through Macy's, I instantly fell in love with it. It went perfectly with my red bucket hat, which I was also wearing. Scrolling through emails on my phone as I waited for my coffee, I felt the pressure of the day catching up with me. Already several new messages. Two from Micah, my boss, one from the graphics department on a design mockup, and a reply from a pastor I had interviewed a couple of months back. Working at a startup magazine was anything but easy, but I loved every second of it. Not only was I a writer and reporter, but my boss, Micah's, go-to person for whatever he needed. Sometimes, it meant donuts and coffee on my way into work, and sometimes, it meant writing ten articles in five days and spot-checking the print run at two o'clock in the morning, four hours before it went to print. It was hard work, but it carried purpose and I thrived on purpose.

"Kirk," the barista said behind the counter, setting a cup down.

It took a moment for the name to register in my mind,

but when it did, my heart leapt as I lifted my eyes to find the face that went with the name. I didn't think about him often, but when he did brush across my thoughts, it was always with fondness for the time we'd shared together on the car trip five years ago. Over the years, the man had stayed with me in the depths of my soul, along with regret. Regret over the fact I hadn't pursued him the day I dropped him off at the bus stop. We hadn't spent time together before our car ride, but the time we did share over the trip was something special and close to my heart still to this day.

Surveying the coffee shop, I held onto the short string of hope I had carried all these years. It was like a loose thread from a piece of clothing that I knew if I pulled, it would unravel the whole thing. I refused to part with it. There was no certainty that Kirk still lived in Spokane, but it didn't stop me from holding onto the possibility. My friend Chloe, back in Albany, hadn't spoken his name in years, understandably, and I'd never found his name on the Spokane Chiefs' roster (I checked every season), but still . . . I refused to part with the string.

"Thanks," a man said, his voice rugged, worn.

Did you enjoy this sample? Pick it up on Amazon today!

ONE THURSDAY MORNING PREVIEW

Prologue

To love and be loved—it was all I ever wanted. Nobody could ever convince me John was a bad man. He made me feel loved when I did not know what love was. I was his and he was mine. It was perfect . . . or at least, I thought it was.

I cannot pinpoint why everything changed in our lives, but it did—and for the worst. My protector, my savior, and my whole world came crashing down like a heavy spring downpour. The first time he struck me, I remember thinking it was just an accident. He had been drinking earlier in the day with his friends and came stumbling home late that night. The lights were low throughout the house because I had already gone to bed. I remember hearing the car pull up outside in the driveway. Leaping to my feet, I came rushing downstairs and through the kitchen to greet him. He swung, which I thought at the time was because I startled him, and the back side of his hand caught my cheek.

I should have known it wasn't an accident.

The second time was no accident at all, and I knew it. After a heavy night of drinking the night his father died, he came to the study where I was reading. Like a hunter looking for his prey, he came up behind me to the couch. Grabbing the back of my head and digging his fingers into my hair, he kinked my neck over the couch and asked me why I hadn't been faithful to him. I had no idea what he was talking about, so out of sheer fear, I began to cry. John took that as a sign of guilt and backhanded me across the face. It was hard enough to leave a bruise the following day. I stayed with him anyway. I'd put a little extra makeup on around my eyes or anywhere else when marks were left. I didn't stay because I was stupid, but because I loved him. I kept telling myself that our love could get us through this. The night of his father's death, I blamed his outburst on the loss of his father. It was too much for him to handle, and he was just letting out steam. I swore to love him through the good times and the bad. This was just one of the bad times.

Each time he'd hit me, I'd come up with a reason or excuse for the behavior. There was always a reason, at least in my mind, as to why John hit me. Then one time, after a really bad injury, I sought help from my mother before she passed away. The closest thing to a saint on earth, she dealt with my father's abuse for decades before he died. She was a devout Christian, but a warped idea of love plagued my mother her entire life. She told me, 'What therefore God hath joined together, let not man put asunder.' That one piece of advice she gave me months before passing made me suffer through a marriage with John for another five trying years.

Each day with John as a husband was a day full of prayer. I would pray for him not to drink, and sometimes, he didn't —those were the days I felt God had listened to my pleas. On the days he came home drunk and swinging, I felt alone, like God had left me to die by my husband's hands. Fear was a cornerstone of our relationship, in my eyes, and I hated it. As the years piled onto one another, I began to deal with two entirely different people when it came to John. There was the John who would give me everything I need in life and bring flowers home on the days he was sober, and then there was John, the drunk, who would bring insults and injury instead of flowers.

I knew something needed to desperately change in my life, but I didn't have the courage. Then one day, it all changed when two little pink lines told me to run and never look back.

Chapter 1

Fingers glided against the skin of my arm as I lay on my side looking into John's big, gorgeous brown eyes. It was morning, so I knew he was sober, and for a moment, I thought maybe, just maybe I could tell him about the baby growing inside me. Flashes of a shared excitement between us blinked through my mind. He'd love having a baby around the house. *He really would.* Behind those eyes, I saw the man I fell in love with years ago down in Town Square in New York City. Those eyes were the same ones that brought me into a world of love and security I had never known before. Moments like that made it hard to hate him. Peering over at his hand that was tracing the side of my body, I saw the cut on his knuckles from where he had smashed the coffee table a few nights ago. My heart retracted the notion of telling him about the baby. I knew John would be dangerous for a child.

Chills shivered up my spine as his fingers traced from my arm to the curve of my back. *Could I be strong enough to live without him?* I wondered as the fears sank back down into me. Even if he was a bit mean, he had a way of charming me like no other man I had ever met in my life. He knew how to touch gently, look deeply and make love passionately. It was only when he drank that his demons came out.

"Want me to make you some breakfast?" I asked, slipping out of his touch and from the bed to my feet. His touches were enjoyable, but I wanted to get used to not having them. My mind often jumped back and forth between leaving, not leaving, and something vaguely in between. It was hard.

John smiled up at me from the bed with what made me feel like love in his eyes. I suddenly began to feel bad about the plan to leave, but I knew he couldn't be trusted with a child. *Keep it together.*

"Sure, babe. That'd be great." He brought his muscular arms from out of the covers and put them behind his head. My eyes traced his biceps and face. Wavy brown hair and a jawline that was defined made him breathtakingly gorgeous. Flashes of last night's passion bombarded my mind. He didn't drink, and that meant one thing—we made love. It started in the main living room just off the foyer. I was enjoying my evening cup of tea while the fireplace was lit when suddenly, John came home early. I was worried at first, but when he leaned over the couch and pulled back my blonde hair, he planted a tender kiss on my neck. I knew right in that moment that it was going to be a good night. Hoisting me up from the couch with those arms and pressing me against the wall near the fireplace, John's passion fell from his lips and onto the skin of my neck as I wrapped my arms around him.

The heat between John and me was undeniable, and it made the thoughts of leaving him that much harder. It was during those moments of pure passion that I could still see the bits of the John I once knew—the part of John that didn't scare me and had the ability to make me feel safe, and the part of him that I never wanted to lose.

"All right," I replied with a smile as I broke away from my thoughts. Leaving down the hallway, I pushed last night out of my mind and focused on the tasks ahead.

Retrieving the carton of eggs from the fridge in the kitchen, I shut the door and was startled when John was standing on the other side. Jumping, I let out a squeak. "John!"

He tilted his head and slipped closer to me. With nothing on but his boxer briefs, he backed me against the counter and let his hand slide the corner of my shirt up my side. He leaned closer to me. I felt the warmth of his breath on my skin as my back arched against the counter top. He licked his lips instinctively to moisten them and then gently let them find their way to my neck. "Serenah . . ." he said in a smooth, seductive voice.

"Let me make you breakfast," I said as I set the carton down on the counter behind me and turned my neck into him to stop the kissing.

His eyebrows rose as he pulled away from my body and released. His eyes met mine. There it was—the change. "*Fine*."

"What?" I replied as I turned and pulled down a frying pan that hung above the island counter.

"Nothing. Nothing. I have to go shower." He left down the hallway without a word, but I could sense tension in his tone.

Waiting for the shower to turn on after he walked into the bathroom and slammed the door, I began to cook his eggs. When a few minutes had passed and I hadn't heard the water start running, I lifted my eyes and looked down the hallway.

There he was.

John stood at the end of hallway, watching me. Standing in the shifting shadows of the long hallway, he was more than creepy. He often did that type of thing, but it came later in the marriage, not early on and only at home. I never knew how long he was standing there before I caught him, but he'd always break away after being seen. He had a sick obsession of studying me like I was some sort of weird science project of his.

I didn't like it all, but it was part of who he had become. *Not much longer,* I reminded myself.

I smiled down the hallway at him, and he returned to the bathroom to finally take his shower. As I heard the water come on, I finished the eggs and set the frying pan off the burner. Dumping the eggs onto a plate, I set the pan in the sink and headed to the piano in the main living room. Pulling the bench out from under the piano, I got down on my hands and knees and lifted the flap of carpet that was squared off. Removing the plank of wood that concealed my secret area, I retrieved the metal box and opened it.

Freedom.

Ever since he hit me that second time, a part of me knew we'd never have the forever marriage I pictured, so in case I was right, I began saving money here and there. I had been able to save just over ten thousand dollars. A fibbed high-priced manicure here, a few non-existent shopping trips with friends there. It added up, and John had not the foggiest clue, since he was too much of an egomaniac to pay attention to anything that didn't directly affect him. Sure, it was his money, but money wasn't really 'a thing' to us. We were beyond that. My eyes looked at the money in the stash and then over at the bus ticket to Seattle dated for four days from now. I could hardly believe it. I was really going to finally leave him after all this time. Amongst the cash and bus ticket, there was a cheap pay-as-you go cellphone and a fake ID. I had to check that box at least once a day ever since I found out about my pregnancy to make sure he hadn't found it. I was scared to leave, but whenever I felt that way, I rubbed my pregnant thirteen-week belly, and I knew I had to do what was best for *us*. Putting the box back into the floor, I was straightening out the carpet when suddenly, John's breathing settled into my ears behind me.

"What are you doing?" he asked, towel draped around his waist behind me. *I should have just waited until he left for work . . . What were you thinking, Serenah?* My thoughts scolded me.

Slamming my head into the bottom of the piano, I grabbed my head and backed out as I let out a groan. "There was a crumb on the carpet."

"What? Underneath the piano?" he asked.

Anxiety rose within me like a storm at sea. Using the bench for leverage, I placed a hand on it and began to get up. When I didn't respond to his question quick enough, he shoved my arm that was propped on the piano bench, causing me to smash my eye into the corner of the bench. Pain radiated through my skull as I cupped my eye and began to cry.

"Oh, please. That barely hurt you."

I didn't respond. Falling the rest of the way to the floor, I cupped my eye and hoped he'd just leave. Letting out a heavy sigh, he got down, still in his towel, and put his hand on my shoulder. "I'm sorry, honey."

Jerking my shoulder away from him, I replied, "Go away!"

He stood up and left.

John hurt me sober? Rising to my feet, I headed into the half-bathroom across the living room and looked into the mirror. My eye was blood red—he had popped a blood vessel. Tears welled in my eyes as my eyebrows furrowed in disgust.

Four days wasn't soon enough to leave—I was leaving today.

Did you enjoy this free sample? Find it on Amazon

FREE GIFT

Cole has fought hundreds of fires in his lifetime, but he had never tasted fear until he came to fighting a fire in his own home. *Amongst The Flames* is a Christian firefighter fiction that tackles real-life situations and problems that exist in Christian marriages today. It brings with it passion, love and spiritual depth that will leave you feeling inspired. This Inspirational Christian romance novel is one book that you'll want to read over and over again.

To Claim Visit:
offer.tkchapin.com

One Sunday Drive (Book 4)

One Monday Prayer (Book 5)

One Tuesday Lunch (Book 6)

One Wednesday Dinner (Book 7)

Embers & Ashes Series

Amongst the Flames (Book 1)

Out of the Ashes (Book 2)

Up in Smoke (Book 3)

After the Fire (Book 4)

Love's Enduring Promise Series

The Perfect Cast (Book 1)

Finding Love (Book 2)

Claire's Hope (Book 3)

Dylan's Faith (Book 4)

Stand Alones

Love Interrupted

Love Again

A Chance at Love

The Broken Road

If Only

Because Of You

The Lies We Believe

In His Love

When It Rains

Gracefully Broken

Please join T.K. Chapin's Mailing List to be notified
of upcoming releases and promotions.

Join the List

ACKNOWLEDGMENTS

First and foremost, I want to thank God. God's salvation through the death, burial and resurrection of Jesus Christ gives us all the ability to have a personal relationship with the Creator of the Universe.

I also want to thank my wife. She's my muse and my inspiration. A wonderful wife, an amazing mother and the best person I have ever met. She's great and has always stood by me with every decision I have made along life's way.

I'd like to thank my editors and early readers for helping me along the way. I also want to thank all of my friends and extended family for the support. It's a true blessing to have every person I know in my life.

ABOUT THE AUTHOR

 **T.K. CHAPIN** writes Christian Romance books designed to inspire and tug on your heart strings. He believes that telling stories of faith, love and family help build the faith of Christians and help non-believers see how God can work in the life of believers. He gives all credit for his writing and storytelling ability to God. The majority of the novels take place in and around Spokane, Washington, his hometown. Chapin makes his home in Idaho and has the pleasure of raising his daughter and two sons with his beautiful wife Crystal.

facebook.com/officialtkchapin

twitter.com/tkchapin

instagram.com/tkchapin